"How *do* you like your men, Sandra?"

She wasn't going to tell Griff, as perhaps he expected from their earlier repartee, that he was her type. She was enjoying this lighthearted encounter, but enough was enough. She didn't want him to get the wrong idea about her. So instead she answered him seriously.

"Kind, home-loving, fond of children, and not so nice-looking that they're conceited about it."

"Just like me, in fact!" Griff settled down in the opposite chair. He swung one long leg negligently over the other, the stretch of his trouser fabric outlining powerful thighs so that Sandra had to avert her gaze determinedly. "Who can tell! With further knowledge, you might find me your *beau idéal*!"

Annabel Murray has pursued many hobbies. She helped found an arts group in Liverpool, England, where she lives with her husband and two daughters. She loves drama: she appeared in many stage productions and went on to write an award-winning historical play. She uses all her experiences—holidays being no exception—to flesh out her characters' backgrounds and create believable settings for her romance novels.

Books by Annabel Murray

HARLEQUIN ROMANCE

8—UNTAMED SANCTUARY
2717—THE COTSWOLD LION
2782—THE PLUMED SERPENT
2819—WILD FOR TO HOLD
2843—RING OF CLADDAGH
2932—HEART'S TREASURE
2952—COLOUR THE SKY RED

HARLEQUIN PRESENTS

933—LAND OF THUNDER
972—FANTASY WOMAN
1029—NO STRINGS ATTACHED
1076—GIFT BEYOND PRICE
1148—A PROMISE KEPT

Sympathetic Strangers

Annabel Murray

Harlequin Books

TORONTO • NEW YORK • LONDON
AMSTERDAM • PARIS • SYDNEY • HAMBURG
STOCKHOLM • ATHENS • TOKYO • MILAN

Original hardcover edition published in 1988
by Mills & Boon Limited

ISBN 0-373-02974-8

Harlequin Romance first edition April 1989

Printed in U.S.A.

CHAPTER ONE

'IT can't be much further now.' Cheerfully, Sandra Tyler reassured her restive young passengers.

Even as she spoke the road took another turn and the North Downs came into view, suffused in late afternoon sunshine. The sight had an extraordinary effect upon her. She was filled with a sense almost of recognition, of homecoming, which was ridiculous. She had never been here before in her life. She pulled the little car into a layby and sat for a few moments just drinking in the beauty of the countryside. Then for the umpteenth time that day she consulted the brand-new road map. Yes, she was on course. Just beyond Godmersham the map showed the route she must take swinging right towards her destination, Vicar's Oak.

She hadn't driven long distances very often and she had a distinct feeling of achievement. In the last few weeks she had made more decisions, tasted more independence than in the whole of her previous life.

'Today,' she said aloud, exultantly, 'is the first day of the rest of my life, and this is a very promising start.'

But despite her sense of euphoria she was tired after the long drive. The twins were weary too. Leo, the more delicate of the pair, was beginning to sound fretful in his demands as to when the journey would be over. As a baby Leo had always been ailing, whereas Anna seemed to have been born with more than her fair share of strength. Seven now, Leo was growing sturdier but he was still less robust than his sister, principally because he was a faddy eater. But Sandra's late husband, Geoffrey, had always maintained that she fussed too much over the child.

Sandra wondered a little anxiously how Leo would adapt to this enormous change to which she was subjecting him. There had already been one major upset in his young life, the loss of his father. Leo's precocious intelligence also made him highly sensitive. He was old enough to dread this mysterious thing called death which made people disappear for ever from his world, but the effect on him had been even more traumatic than she had feared. She wasn't so worried about Anna, she thought, with an amused affectionate glance at her daughter. The little girl was as intelligent but more placid and less imaginative then her twin. Leo's ordeals were Anna's adventures. Some people might think she should not have uprooted her young family, that they should have stayed in familiar surroundings a little longer. But Sandra was sure she was doing the right thing.

And this was enchanted country, she thought. Her fatigue lifted as she drove on, as the road became a winding, undulating country lane. Away from the steady thrum and harsh glisten of speeding traffic she was better able to appreciate the scenery. A copse of stately pale-foliaged beeches drew her beauty-loving eyes to wide horizons. A hump-backed bridge beckoned to those with time to spare to follow it over a meandering stream, past a watermill to a lush meadow where cattle stood belly-deep in buttercups. And were those hop gardens?

She hadn't expected to find hops growing this far east. Throughout Kent she had seen many oasthouses, whole clusters of them, thrusting upward temple-like amid spring blossom. But here was that distinctive shape again giving a foreign aspect to the landscape. She could see women working in the fields among the spring shoots, training them to climb gigantic cat's cradles of string between the permanent poles and wires.

The road wound on. Then, after a particularly sharp bend, 'Mummy, are we nearly there?' This time it was Anna, not fretful but characteristically practical. 'Leo's feeling sick!'

'Oh, no!' Sandra cried. She braked sharply. When Leo felt travel-sick immediate action was called for.

The Land Rover, travelling at speed, swung around the bend and came suddenly upon the small car which obstructed the road, both doors wide open. The vehicle had apparently been abandoned by its occupants. The driver braked hard and the Land Rover slithered to a sideways halt only inches from the bumper of the stationary car.

'Damn and blast it! What a bloody stupid place to stop!'

He had begun the day in a slightly happier mood than he had felt of late. He wasn't particularly superstitious about such things but he might have known the feeling wouldn't last. He swung long legs clad in disreputable jeans from behind the wheel of the Land Rover and stalked across the grass verge. The fact that the offender was one of the most striking women he had seen in a long time did nothing to lessen his annoyance. Even so he registered the sweet madonna-like quality of her oval face, an impression heightened by the fall of brown hair, straight as a veil, curving only at the long, pure jawline.

Sandra, busy comforting her unhappy small son,

was unaware of the commotion going on behind her, but with her usual phlegmatic calm her daughter had assessed the situation.

'Mummy, that Land Rover nearly crashed into us. The man looks very cross.'

A distracted glance over her shoulder assured Sandra that 'the man' was indeed annoyed and that he was now striding towards them, his approach made all the more menacing by his considerable height and breadth of shoulder.

'Oh, Lord,' Sandra breathed the words apprehensively. 'That's all I need!' Quite likely he saw her as a 'Sunday afternoon motorist' as her late husband had been used to say scornfully of any driver who incurred his displeasure.

'Do you realise you could have caused a very nasty accident?' As she had feared, once within earshot the tall man wasted no time. A strong clean-shaven jaw was set with displeasure. 'Don't you know any better than to stop just around a bend? Blocking the whole road, too. And suppose I'd crashed into the back of you? Suppose your children had still been in the car? They might have been killed.'

Did he *have* to be quite so ferocious? Sandra thought indignantly. Then she took a deep breath as her innate sense of fairness reminded her that he had some justification for his annoyance. She had been rather careless in forsaking the car just at that point.

'They wouldn't have been in the car,' she pointed out in a tone of quiet reason. 'I stopped because they had to get out. My son has just been very sick.'

At once the widely spaced green eyes softened and his whole expression changed as he turned towards the woebegone Leo. He went down on his haunches beside the little boy, who flinched away and looked for reassurance from Sandra.

'Poor old chap,' the man said sympathetically. 'How rotten. I used to have the same trouble at your age.' To Sandra, he said, 'Sorry I sounded off like that. I appreciate your problem. It's just that I wasn't expecting to come upon a stationary vehicle just there, and I must confess my mind was on other things.' Sandra gathered from his expression that his thoughts hadn't been pleasant ones and she felt a twinge of sympathy. Whatever it was must have been bad to make those splendid green eyes so suddenly bleak. 'I suppose you could say I'm a bit sensitive about motor accidents just at the present moment.' So that was it.

'I'm sorry too.' Warm grey eyes in an oval face too long for conventional beauty looked up earnestly at him. 'Normally I'm a very careful driver,' she assured him. 'But when Leo feels sick, there isn't much time before . . .' She grimaced comically, inviting him to share her amusement as she felt a strange compulsion to banish that stricken look of his. 'Well, let's say you have to act fast. We've just had a long, tiring journey from the other side of London.' Then to Leo, her expression one of tender concern, 'Feeling better, darling? It really isn't much further now.'

'Where are you headed?' The tall man loped beside her as she walked towards the car, Leo's hot little hand still tightly clutching hers.

'Vicar's Oak. Do you know it? The last signpost said it was only another five miles.'

'Hmmph. Five miles of very twisting, bumpy lanes. Why not let the children ride with me? My vehicle is better fitted for this type of road than yours.'

Sandra regarded him doubtfully. He might be one of the most striking-looking men she had ever encountered, and friendly now that his anger had passed, but let her children drive away with a total stranger? The expression in her almond-shaped grey eyes gave him her answer without the need for words.

'Look,' he said drily, 'I'm not trying to abduct them. Heaven forbid I should want to saddle myself with somebody else's kids. I've trouble enough of my own. I was merely trying to be helpful. And you'll find I'm well known in Vicar's Oak.'

'I'm sure you are,' she said hastily, 'but really, no thank you. Leo, Anna, get back in the car, then I can move it out of the way.'

A shrug of his broad shoulders disposed of her, her children and her problems, and Sandra felt an unexpectedly strong sense of disappointment when, without another word, he strode towards his own vehicle. And as she restarted her engine and moved the car into the side of the road, the Land Rover surged past and disappeared from view around the next bend.

'He reminded me of Daddy,' Anna said.

'He wasn't a bit like Daddy!' Sandra exclaimed in surprise. Geoffrey had been stockily built, fair-haired, exceedingly handsome. Leo would take after him some day.

The stranger had been far from handsome, though he wasn't exactly ugly, she reflected. But he was tall, several inches taller than Geoffrey had been, and his hair was a most attractive shade of bronze, somewhere between the richness of horse chestnuts and the glinting patina of copper. Like the twins Geoffrey's eyes had been blue. This man's eyes had been a strange, cat-like shade of green. And Geoffrey wouldn't have been seen dead in those scruffy jeans and equally ancient pullover. It was surprising, she thought, amused at herself, just how much she *had* noticed about the man.

'No,' she repeated, 'he wasn't a bit like Daddy.'

'He didn't look like him,' Anna agreed, 'but when he was cross to start with he sounded just like him. When he used to get mad with you.'

Sandra winced painfully. It was worrying sometimes just how perceptive children could be. She and Geoffrey had had their disagreements even before she had found out he was deceiving her with his beautiful, sophisticated secretary. But she *had* tried, if not always successfully, to protect the children from any ugliness in their relationship. And Anna was right. Geoffrey had been used to speak abruptly to her. Only his manner had been far worse, scornfully denigrating, always belittling her. The recollection still hurt even though he had killed her love for him long ago. If she had been the neurotic type, she thought, he might even have convinced her totally of her worthlessness. But she was made of sterner stuff than that, thank goodness.

'No, he wasn't like Daddy,' Leo joined in the discussion. 'Daddy used to say only cissies were travel-sick. I rather liked that man.' From the cautious Leo that was quite something.

'Well, I *didn't* like him,' Anna retorted. The twins rarely argued, but when they did . . . Sandra decided it was time to put an end to the discussion.

'Oh, well,' she said cheerfully, 'I don't suppose we're likely to meet him again. Even though he comes from Vicar's Oak, I shouldn't think he's one of Aunt Nonie's friends.' There had been a distinct air about him, what Sandra's mother would have termed 'quality'. Sandra had no time for snobbery, but Dorothy Lessing had been brought up in an age when more class consciousness existed. But Sandra's mother had other, sometimes more inconvenient traits, one of which was the cause of Sandra's present journey.

One of Dorothy's idiosyncrasies was a busy social conscience which caused her to involve herself deeply in the affairs of others. Her mother's impetuosity was a long-standing family joke. Geoffrey had laughed with the rest. But he had always been at pains to ensure that Sandra didn't take after her mother.

Following the death of her husband and his mistress in a road accident, Sandra had welcomed the twins' Easter holidays as a chance to get out of London and out of the flat which held only oppressive memories of her marriage. She had taken the twins to visit her parents in Hertfordshire. The children, Leo in particular, needed their thoughts diverting from the recent tragedy, while Sandra herself had felt she could do with a breathing-space in which to consider her future and that of the twins.

It had been tremendously enjoyable having her son and daughter to herself for two weeks without the hovering presence of the nanny her late husband had insisted on for his children. Geoffrey had never wanted a family in the first place. His wife had to be available to fit in with his every whim. As an only child Sandra had gone straight from a happy family life and her natural dependence on her parents into dependence on her husband. Geoffrey Tyler had attempted to mould her to his ways. He had directed every aspect of her life. And because she'd loved him she'd allowed it to happen. She had realised her mistakes too late.

Now, she thought with a sense of guilty relief, she could please herself, about her children's upbringing, and about other things. Geoffrey had left her very well off. But the idea of continuing what she considered to be the useless butterfly existence she had led with him appalled her. She would get a job, something her husband hadn't permitted. The only problem was, having married young, she had never trained for anything. She had left school with excellent A-levels and until she had met Geoffrey Tyler she'd been all set to train as a children's nurse.

Her parents hadn't been too keen on her early marriage or on her husband-to-be, but she had never told them they'd been correct in their doubts. They would only have worried, and she would have felt disloyal.

'Mummy! Mummy! You've just passed a sign that said Vicar's Oak,' practical little Anna told her. 'You're going the wrong way!'

Sandra negotiated a tricky three-point turn in the narrow lane.

'What would I do without you two?' She smiled at the twins affectionately.

The twins' Easter holidays had been drawing swiftly to an end and Sandra had been no nearer a decision about her future when her mother received a letter from her old friend, Leonora Hartoch, known to those who loved her as Nonie. Three years ago Nonie, a widow, had gone to keep house for her nephew, the Reverend Dorian Hartoch. Amber, his wife of eighteen months, who sounded a highly unsuitable partner for a clergyman, had apparently been having an affair with a well-to-do local man called Faversham and was in his car when it was involved in a crash. Amber had been badly hurt and was now confined to a wheelchair, perhaps permanently.

Dorothy Lessing had telephoned her friend and had been all for rushing down to Kent to help out. For as well as acting as his housekeeper, Nonie Hartoch assisted her nephew with his parish activities. The additional task of caring for an invalid was proving to be too much of a strain and on a country vicar's stipend the Hartochs could not afford paid help.

But having telephoned, Dorothy, who led a hectic life herself, realised she was too heavily committed over the next few weeks to be able to leave home.

On an impulse Sandra offered to go down to Kent instead of her mother, seeing this in any case as a heaven-sent excuse not to go back to London.

'Are you sure you can cope?' her mother had asked anxiously.

But this only put Sandra on her mettle. Somehow she had always coped. She had coped with even Geoffrey's most impossible demands. She had coped when her husband, an energetic and successful businessman, had landed her with unexpected last-minute guests. No one had ever been allowed to guess at the tremulous, uncertain girl beneath the quietly efficient, well-dressed young hostess Geoffrey expected her to be. His business associates and their hard-boiled glamorous wives had never known how much she disliked the continual travelling in England and overseas, the glossy hotels, the insincere, brittle conversation. No, she had never let Geoffrey down. But in the end, she thought, her mouth twisted, *he* had let *her* down. Oh, she could sympathise with Dorian Hartoch over his wife's defection.

'I'll cope,' she'd said firmly. 'I'd like to see Aunt Nonie again. It's been years. And if it doesn't work out there'll be no real harm done. I'd planned to get out of London anyway, so the twins would have been changing schools eventually. And the country air will be good for them. Leo always looks so peaky in town.'

Sandra had never been to Kent. It would be something new and surely she wouldn't be expected to spend all her time with Amber Hartoch. She and the twins could go exploring. She made rapid mental plans, to give Nanny her marching orders, to dispose of the flat, and for the purchase of a smaller vehicle. Geoffrey had insisted on her learning to drive and there had been a second car for her use. But, like all Geoffrey's ideas, it had been too large for her. She didn't like big, fast cars. A small family runabout was all she and the twins would need.

'Mummy! This is it. We're here!' Leo had survived the remaining distance to Vicar's Oak without futher mishap.

The village was edged by cottages doddering with age, yet trim and flowery. Sandra had no difficulty in identifying the tall rather austere-looking vicarage standing in the shadow of a somewhat unprepossessing church. Her heart sank a little as she observed the vicarage's lack of front garden, the overgrown churchyard. She had promised the children lovely countryside and that had materialised. But she had also promised them a nice home and garden where, unlike in the flat, they would have plenty of room to run free.

But she cheered up considerably as she observed the crisp whiteness of the window nets, the pristine paintwork of the front door, the shining brass of the old-fashioned knocker. Then the door was thrown open and she and the twins were engulfed in the warmth of Nonie's welcome.

'Sandra? It is Sandra? Of course it is. I think I should have known you anywhere, even though it must be all of fifteen years. You're so like dear Dottie. And these are the twins, bless them. But come in, come in. You must be worn out after your journey and after all you've had to do in so little time. I'm so grateful to you for coming here at such short notice.'

No wonder Leonora Hartoch and Dorothy Lessing had got on so well. They were two of a kind, Sandra thought as the older woman rattled on. When they were together it must have been difficult for either woman to get a word in.

'I was sorry to hear about your husband.' Nonie led the way into a large surprisingly homely kitchen. 'I hope you don't mind, but the parlour's so formal. We only use it for seeing the parishioners. What happened to Geoffrey, dear? Your mother didn't say. Just that you'd lost him and needed a change. Was it an accident?'

'Yes,' with a wary glance at the twins. Death was a touchy subject with them just at the moment—with Leo in particular. 'A car crash.'

'Just like Amber's. Well . . .' with pursed lips, 'not *just* like. Dear, oh dear, the harm motorists can do. I'm glad I never learnt to drive.'

'*We* nearly had a crash,' Anna confided. She was not a shy child. In fact Sandra rather deplored her daughter's indiscriminate friendships.

'Did you, pet?' Nonie's grey eyebrows lifted questioningly at Sandra over the child's head.

'Yes, a man with a Land Rover nearly ran into the back of us. He was very cross with Mummy.'

'It's all right, Aunt Nonie,' Sandra said quickly. 'There was no damage done. The man was a bit annoyed at first. But he had some justification.' But as she explained the circumstances she recalled that momentary antagonism she had felt towards the tall man.

'Poor Leo,' Nonie said sympathetically. 'But who was this man? Did he give you his name?'

'No.'

'Well, what was he like?'

Sandra had a sudden image, startling in its detail of that unconventional face, the widely spaced vivid green eyes. And for some reason she shivered.

'He said everybody in Vicar's Oak knew him,' Anna volunteered.

'Well, in that case you're bound to meet him again, Sandra dear. We're quite a small community. Everybody knows everyone else. Quite a lot of people own Land Rovers. Dorian has one himself. They're more suitable for country lanes.'

Nonie suggested they might all like to see their bedrooms before they ate.

'I've put the twins in together. Is that all right?'

'Yes. They're pretty well inseparable. Oh, what a lovely room!' Sandra's reaction was one of genuine admiration but also one of relief. Inside the house was certainly much more attractive than its unprepossessing exterior.

'Yes, isn't it? Dorian's worked so hard these last three years to make a nice home for us, and more recently of course for his wife. He has plans next for the church and the churchyard, which both sadly need attention. You know, dear, as his aunt I'm bound to be prejudiced, but he really is the most admirable man.'

It would be interesting, Sandra thought with some amusement, to renew her acquaintance with Nonie's paragon of a nephew whom she vaguely recollected as a shock-headed youth with unusually vivid eyes.

'I was so pleased when he got this living and asked me to keep house for him,' Nonie chattered on as Sandra unpacked for herself and the twins. 'And when he got married he said I mustn't even think of leaving.

Amber didn't seem to mind me staying on and it was all working out so well, until Amber started running round with her county friends. And then of course there was the accident.'

Alone at last, Sandra freshened up, washed the twins and put them into very necessary clean clothes. This done, they all descended to the kitchen once more where a splendid high tea awaited them.

'Dorian and Amber are out,' Nonie explained. 'He had some errands so he took her to her grandmother's in Dartford and left her there for the afternoon and evening. He thought it might be an ordeal for you to have to meet them straight away.'

Leo, as usual, had to be coaxed into making a good meal, while his sister stolidly munched her way through sandwiches, home-made scones and cakes.

'The country air will improve his appetite,' Nonie observed comfortingly.

'I certainly wish something would,' Sandra said, an anxious little frown between her eyes, as her son, released from the table, urged his twin to hurry up so that they could go and play the old harmonium they had discovered in the parlour. 'I worry about him rather a lot.'

'Best not to force him, dear,' Nonie advised when the children were out of earshot. 'It only makes them more stubborn. He'll come to it all in his own good time.'

Later, with the twins safely tucked away in bed, Sandra was able to talk more freely with the woman for whom 'aunt' was merely a courtesy title. As Nonie had said, it was a long time since they had met. On the last occasion Sandra had been little more than a child.

As a young woman, Leonora Hartoch must have been very attractive, Sandra mused, as she watched

Nonie move around the large homely kitchen making a fresh pot of tea. Now, just turned seventy, she still had a serene beauty. Her iron-grey hair was immaculately styled in a bob with a heavy wave that constantly fell over one eye and was as constantly pushed back. Steel-rimmed glasses framed eyes that were surprisingly clear-sighted. Only the slight crêpiness of her hands betrayed that she was older than she looked.

'And how are your dear parents?' Nonie asked when she finally sat down.

'Very well. As busy as ever. Dad with his landscape-gardening business and Mum with her committees. She's never still.'

'Dear Dorothy,' Nonie laughed. 'That comes from her upbringing as a clergyman's daughter. You know her father, your grandfather, had the next parish to my late husband?'

'Yes.' Sandra had heard the story many times from her mother. 'And Mum was your chief bridesmaid and met Dad at your wedding.'

'Now tell me about yourself,' Nonie invited. 'You know, dear, you look scarcely old enough to be the mother of seven-year-old children.'

'There's not a lot to tell,' Sandra confessed, her grey eyes wistful. 'I'm afraid I'm a very uninteresting sort of person. I'm twenty-six. I was married young, almost straight out of school, and I had the twins right away.'

'But you and your husband led a very busy, interesting life?'

'Yes, but it wasn't really me. I felt I was putting on an act all the time.' Sandra was surprised to find herself confiding in the older woman something she had never dreamed of telling her parents. 'I know I was a disappointment to Geoff. I'm not a jet-setter. I would much rather have been just a housewife. And I would have loved a garden.' Sandra had inherited her love of gardening from her father. As a teenager she had often helped him with his projects.

'There's plenty of garden here,' Nonie told her with a rueful smile, and at Sandra's look of surprise, 'at the back of the house. Far too much for us to manage. And it's grown very wild, like the churchyard. But I dare say the children will love it. Did Dorothy tell you there's a very good progressive school over in Filberton, the next village? So you needn't worry about that.'

The snobbish Geoffrey, Sandra thought, would have been horrified at the thought of his children going to a country village school no one had heard of. Such considerations didn't weigh with her as long as the standard of education was good. Sandra's only fear concerning bringing the twins to Kent had been that the older woman might find the presence of two small children an additional trial. But Nonie declared herself delighted to have them.

'I never had any family of my own, you know, and I love to make a fuss of other people's children.' It was not so much physical stress she was feeling as mental, she declared.

'The atmosphere between Dorian and Amber is very strained. And I'm in the middle of it all. But tell me, my dear, what do you plan to do with yourself, after you've so very kindly helped us?'

'I honestly don't know. Originally I'd planned to be a children's nurse. Now I'm not sure I could devote sufficient time to studying. Because I cetainly don't want another Nanny for the twins. I'd rather look after them myself.' She smiled, and the effort struck the older woman as being a particularly gallant one.

'Whenever I was unhappy in my marriage I used to remind myself that without marriage I'd never have had the twins. And I wouldn't be without them for the world.'

'It sounds to me,' Nonie said sagely, 'that what would make you happiest would be a comfortable domestic life, looking after your home and children. Perhaps you'll get married again some day.'

'I'd certainly like to think so,' Sandra agreed. Then, 'Does that sound heartless?' Her grey eyes were anxious. 'It isn't meant to. Whatever Geoffrey and I had was finished, long ago, even before his accident. But,' she sighed, 'who'd want to marry a woman who already has two children? And though I love being a mother, I honestly don't think I'm very good at being a wife. I wasn't the sort Geoffrey needed anyway.' Her outward show of sophistication had not deceived his critical eyes.

'Nonsense!' Nonie exclaimed. 'From what your mother tells me you've always been splendid. And I refuse to believe that a lovely young woman like you won't be snapped up sooner or later by some discerning man. What a pity,' she said in the tones of one who has just made an amazing discovery, 'what a pity Dorian isn't free. You and he would get on splendidly.'

Sandra smiled. She had already discovered that Nonie was partial about her nephew and guessed that the older woman welcomed any opportunity to talk about him.

'Tell me about Dorian,' she encouraged her, 'and about his wife, of course.'

'You'll soon find out about Dorian for yourself. He's a good man, hard-working and transparently honest. But Amber? As to her character, a flighty girl

I'm afraid. And her health, well, there *is* just a chance she may recover. She has to see the specialist again in six months when her nervous system has had a chance to settle down.'

'And if she doesn't recover?' Sandra asked. 'What then?'

'Well, then,' Nonie sighed. 'I suppose we'll have to find somebody permanent. But by that time there should be some insurance money. Naturally Amber's very depressed,' and as Sandra shook her head sympathetically, she added tartly, 'not very sweet-tempered either. Oh, yes, Amber's a very different kettle of fish.'

'Don't you like her, Aunt Nonie?' It couldn't be easy for Nonie Hartoch to see her adored nephew married to someone of whom she disapproved.

'I don't dislike her, dear. Not even now, when . . . But to be honest I never felt she was the right wife for Dorian. Too young, too wild, too wilful and far too restless ever to settle down to parish routine. But men can be quite unreasonable when they're in love. And look what's happened. I suppose Dorothy told you about Amber's involvement with young Faversham.'

The sound of a vehicle drawing up outside interrupted Nonie and brought her to her feet.

'That will be Dorian and Amber. They're earlier than I expected.'

Sandra rose too.

'Would you mind very much if I slipped away? Before they come in? I'm tired and I . . .'

'And you'd rather meet them in the morning when you're rested? I quite understand, my dear, and I know Dorian will.'

Though she was tired, Sandra was still able to look around her with interest. Dorian had been busy in this room too. Modern plumbing had been installed. The beige and brown décor was tasteful to her tired eyes. Colour had been added in the rose-pink bedcover and curtains.

She had expected to fall asleep immediately. But the events of the day were still too vivid, keeping her brain active. It had happened before on the rare occasions when she had driven a long way, as though the vigilant part of her brain could not relax. But it was not the details of the journey which kept her wakeful, but the encounter with the tall driver of the Land Rover. She found she just could not get his face out of her mind so that it was some time before she drifted into an uneasy slumber and to her shame she overslept next morning.

'Oh, heavens! I'm so sorry! This is no way to help you,' she told Nonie when the older woman woke her with a breakfast tray. But Nonie swept aside her guilty apologies.

'Yesterday must have been quite a strain for you. That long drive. And you're not to worry about the twins. They're up and dressed and exploring the garden.'

But Sandra was still dismayed by her own tardiness.

'Whatever must Dorian and Amber think of me?'

'My dear, Amber doesn't like to be roused until just before midday and Dorian's been out since the small hours. One of his parishioners is dying. He won't be back until it's all over.'

Despite Nonie's reassurances, Sandra made a rapid breakfast. She showered and dressed in an all-purpose outfit of faded jeans and an old shirt, then went downstairs ready for whatever chores she might be asked to do. Carrying her breakfast tray she made her way to the kitchen, but stopped short on its threshold.

Involuntarily her eyes had widened and she was aware of an unaccountable breathlessness.

'Good heavens! What are *you* doing here?' she exclaimed.

It was the man from yesterday, the driver of the Land Rover. He had been sitting at his ease in a chair near the open fire, lit to offset the chilly spring weather. But at the sight of Sandra he rose to his full height and as she stared at him, once again she was very much aware that this man, though not handsome, was by no means ugly. He had an interesting face. His mouth was perhaps his most attractive feature with its long top lip and fuller, sensual lower one. It had a permanent uplift to the corners as though he smiled at secrets only he perceived.

'What are *you* doing *here?*' she asked again.

'I might ask you the same thing!' he rejoined lazily. 'Except that I have the advantage of you. You're Sandra, aren't you? Nonie's saviour?' He watched with amusement as the almond-shaped grey eyes widened still further.

'You're not . . .' Sandra was aware of disproportionate dismay. 'Oh, you can't be Dorian Hartoch?'

CHAPTER TWO

'NOW do I *look* like a clergyman?' As he studied her incredulous face he seemed inordinately amused about something.

Her fascinated gaze followed the downward sweep of a large hand, over the beige rolled-necked sweater and faded brushed denims. But it wasn't the clothes that influenced her reply. In her experience clergymen did not appraise an unknown woman in that openly bold fashion which seemed to penetrate her clothing, assessing the femininity beneath.

'No,' she answered with the downright frankness that characterised her nature and of which Geoffrey had tried in vain to cure her. 'You certainly don't look like a clergyman or behave like one. I take it that means you're not?'

'Doesn't that mean you *hope* not?' he countered and he grinned quizzically, apparently unabashed by her disapproving manner. 'Would it be so disastrous, Sandra, to find yourself living under the same roof as me?'

She hadn't meant it that way at all. But for some reason, it *was* a relief to find he wasn't Dorian Hartoch. She didn't try to analyse her reactions but hovered, tray in hand, wanting to get to the sink but oddly reluctant to move past the dauntingly large figure.

Of course it wouldn't be disastrous.' She blurted out the words, then realised what she'd said, how it might sound, or rather how he might decide to take it, and she blushed furiously. She sought frantically for a change of subject. 'I am sorry about yesterday. And I hope you didn't think me rude, refusing your offer to take the twins, but . . .' She stopped. Geoffrey would have said she was talking too much, too fast, just like her mother.

'Now there's a rarity!' The green eyes were still amused by something. 'A woman apologising to me. It's usually the other way about. Most of the women I know go into the self-justification routine as a matter of course. And if they're proved wrong, they sulk.' His smile took any offence out of the words and suddenly Sandra found herself grinning back, liking him.

'I can only suggest,' she said with calculated demureness, 'that you alter your circle of acquaintance.'

'I see.' He folded his arms across a broad chest and leant against the kitchen table, his face composed into lines of serious attention belied by the glint in his eyes. 'What would you suggest then? That I further my acquaintance with you, perhaps?'

A bubble of laughter welled up inside her. This was fun. And Sandra realised just how long it was since a personable man had flirted with her. But, she thought guiltily, she was here to work and she still hadn't got a clue who he was or what he was doing in the vicarage kitchen. She didn't even know if he had any right to be there.

'Excuse me.' She raised the tray slightly as indication of her desire to get on with some washing up.

The tray was deftly removed from her hands and placed on the spotless drainer. Meanwhile he smiled down into eyes heavily fringed with dark lashes, which had widened involuntarily at the inadvertent brush of his fingers on hers.

'Suppose,' he suggested, 'that you leave that until I've apologised again for my brusqueness yesterday and you've made us both a coffee.'

'Actually,' she told him a little incoherently, 'I've only just had my breakfast and a whole pot of tea, so I don't really want a coffee. But if you . . .'

'Yes, I do,' the deep voice cajoled. 'Nonie would have made me one by now if she were here, but she isn't. And I'd rather you joined me.' A touch of pathos which signally failed to convince. 'It's rather lonely drinking alone.'

'I'm very busy. What's wrong with you making one for yourself?' Sandra said cheekily, making an attempt to sidestep him, an attempt which was foiled once more, this time by a large pair of hands which clamped firmly on her shoulders. The contact had the oddest effect on her. It took her breath away and sent a warm glow through her veins, flooding her entire being with an awareness of his masculinity, an awareness that held a strange element of fear.

'You don't look all that busy. Besides I don't take liberties in other people's kitchens.'

'No?' Sandra was determined not to reveal the upheaval he had caused within her. She smiled, raised her eyebrows and glanced meaningly from shoulder to shoulder. But the implied reproof was ineffective, so she looked up at him instead, then had to make a valiant attempt to hold the bold gaze of the vivid green eyes. 'So you're not Dorian,' was the only coherent thing she could think of to say.

'No, I'm not,' he agreed. 'I'm Griff. And since you obviously have revolutionary ideas about woman's place in the kitchen, with your permission I *will* make that coffee for both of us.' So saying, he pressed her down into the chair he had only recently vacated. It gave Sandra a curious feeling of intimacy to find the cushions still warm with the impress of his large frame and she felt an almost irresistible impulse to curl up cat-like in the chair and luxuriate in the sensation. 'So you're Sandra,' he said as he found his way around the kitchen with a suspicious ease, which made her guess he had done so many times before. 'And you're really the mother of those twins? Incredible! How old are they?'

'Seven!'

'And your husband? Where's he?'

'My husband died, two months ago, in a motoring accident.' As on that previous occasion when accidents had been referred to she thought she saw a flicker of some emotion cloud the green eyes for a moment, but then the expression was gone.

'A widow,' he said thoughtfully. 'A grieving one?' In anyone else the question would have smacked of insensitivity, but he sounded genuinely interested, concerned.

'What would you expect?' Sandra said evasively. She regretted Geoffrey's death as she would have regretted any other. But her grief was not that of a woman mourning a much-loved husband. And a stranger might not understand.

'Oh, I don't know.' The humour was back in his face. 'Some wives consider themselves well rid of their husbands.'

'And vice versa,' she retorted gamely but giving nothing away. 'Have you a wife?' She was curiously eager for his answer.

'Do you think *she* would be well rid of *me* ?' Amusement fired the green eyes. 'I've nearly made it to the altar a couple of times, as it happens. But I've yet to find the woman who'll fit in with my life-style.' The words struck a chill, reminding her with distaste of Geoffrey's attitude. 'No, I'm not married. Though everyone, including Nonie, keeps telling me it's time I was. But I don't believe in getting married just for the sake of it, do you?'

'No,' she agreed with feeling. 'There's an awful lot to take into consideration.'

'Such as? You're very vehement.' He sounded interested but Sandra couldn't see why he should want to hear her views on the subject.

'Far too much to list,' she said with a smile as he handed her the cup of coffee he had made anyway, and she found after all that she did want it, almost as if she needed something to steady her.

'Not too strong for you?'

'Actually,' she sipped appreciatively, 'I like my coffee strong.'

'Like your men? Isn't that how the saying goes?' And as she smiled non-committally, 'How *do* you like your men, Sandra?'

She wasn't going to tell him, as perhaps he expected from their earlier repartee, that *he* was her type. She was enjoying this light-hearted encounter, but enough was enough. She didn't want him to get the wrong idea about her. So instead she answered him seriously.

'Kind, home-loving, fond of children, and not so nice looking that they're conceited about it.'

'Just like me, in fact!' He settled down in the opposite chair. One long leg swung negligently over the other, the stretch of his trouser fabric outlining powerful thighs so that Sandra had to avert her gaze determinedly. 'Who can tell? With further knowledge,

you might find *me* your *beau idéal!*'
Sandra was aware again of that strange breathlessness. Despite his unconventional looks, this man had an undoubtedly masculine attraction which was having its effect on her. But she had been swayed by considerations of that kind before. Besides, goodness, whatever was she thinking of? She didn't want to turn into one of those women who viewed every new man they met as a possible mate.
'So am I to be given a chance to prove myself?' He might still be joking. But if he was serious things were going a bit too fast for her. And it meant she had given him a wrong impression.
'I really must get on with some work.' She rose quickly, shaking off the bemusement into which he seemed to have cast her. She drained the coffee too quickly, burning her mouth, then carried her cup to the sink where she began a show of being busy, clattering pots. 'I'm here to help look after Mrs Hartoch—Amber,' she told him. 'You know her, of course.'
'Of course!' The deep voice carried more than a hint of irony. 'Who doesn't know Amber? And you think she's more in need of your society than I am?' Dismayed, she found he had moved to stand close beside her, and to her astonishment he picked up a tea-towel.
'You don't look to me to be the sort of man who'd lack for companionship.' She tried to sound casual, detached, and as though her pulses had not responded erratically to the warmth of his proximity. Carefully she made sure there was no accidental contact between them as he took the wet plates straight from her hand.
'Oh?' interestedly. 'Now I wonder exactly what you

mean by that? Do I take it you're asking if I'm short of female companionship, by any chance?'

A cup nearly slipped through her fingers. Sandra knew she was becoming flustered. And he was too astute. She emptied the plastic washing-up bowl and began to attack the sink with cloth, scouring powder and ferocious energy.

'If that's what you were implying,' he persisted, 'I suppose I should be flattered. Since it must indicate your belief that women would find me attractive?'

Sandra remained doggedly silent. He really was incorrigibly complacent.

'Do you find me attractive, Sandra?' He bent to peer into her face, which by now was rather pink and warm.

'I hadn't thought about it.' But that wasn't true. Throughout this ridiculous conversation it had been impossible not to be aware of a certain magnetism, an overt masculinity that pulled disastrously at her senses. It was too soon, she scolded herself, to feel that way about a total stranger. Next time, if there was a next time, she wanted to know a man really well before she fell for him. And she knew exactly the kind of man she would be looking for.

'Why not give it some thought now?' he suggested. The tea-towel discarded he moved in on her, his hands grasping her shoulders once more. Their bodies were almost touching and his head was lowered towards her in an alarming way that made her pulses leap, her heart skitter, so that her breast rose and fell on an unsteady breath.

'Please . . . Mr . . . Griff.' She was amazed that her voice sounded so calm. 'Please let go of me. I don't know how the other women you know would behave but I . . .' If he moved even slightly he would brush against her. The knowledge added to her already considerable agitation sending tremors through her stomach. If that happened she might not be able to hide her surging awareness of him.

'You're not even the slightest bit interested?' His keen eyes had not missed the disturbance to her breathing, the pulse that leapt frantically at the base of her throat. 'You wouldn't permit me to put that to the test, I suppose?'

'No!' She panicked and wrenched free of him. The frank friendliness, the gamine sense of humour, of which Geoffrey had been unable to break her, had got her into this situation. She succeeded in putting the large kitchen table between them and they stood on either side of it, her gaze watchful, wary, his warmly amused, intensely interested. And it was as if she had not freed herself from his grasp. The thread of tension between them was as palpable as when those strong, hard fingers had startled and warmed her soft flesh.

'You're afraid to let me try!' he accused, amusement lighting his eyes.

'No!' she denied mendaciously. 'It's not that. I . . .' Suddenly she wished her faded old jeans did not cling quite so smoothly to her hips and thighs, that she had replaced the missing top button on her blouse. Without thinking, she put up her hand to cover the deficiency, saw him note her reaction and his amusement deepen. She bent her head, letting a veil of soft brown hair mask her embarrassment.

'Sandra,' there was an oddly caressive note in the way he said her name, 'is it because we didn't exactly get off on the right foot yesterday? I have apologised for that.'

'Oh, no!' Honesty made her gaze direct once more. She couldn't let him think her capable of such pettiness. 'But I think you've misunderstood. I don't know you from Adam and,' with more than a trace of indignation, 'I'm not used to such familiarity from a total stranger.'

He didn't reply at first, but studied her closely almost as if, she thought, she were an unfamiliar species to him. Perhaps she was. Perhaps most women fell willingly into his arms.

'Point taken,' he said evenly. 'But I hope we shan't always be strangers, Sandra. And I'm sorry if I was wrong in thinking we might take a few short cuts. Because I have a feeling we could be friends—very *good* friends, perhaps?'

'I don't know.' She moved around, straightening crockery on the old-fashioned Welsh dresser, fidgeting unnecessarily with tea-towels, anything to avoid facing him. Suddenly it was impossible to remain still under his gaze. 'I'm not here to socialise, you know.' But something within her felt an intense curiosity as to how it would be to be this man's companion, to know his touch, his kiss. Afraid her thoughts might show in her face, Sandra continued, 'I'm here to help Nonie. What with that and the twins to look after there won't be time for anything else.'

'If you think that,' drily, 'then you don't know Nonie. I'll lay even money before a week is out she'll have you involved in parish activities. And I see no reason why your good works shouldn't extend to keeping a lonely bachelor company occasionally.' The note of mock pathos was back she noted. 'Care to bet on it?' he invited. He had settled himself in a chair again looking as if he were there for the duration.

'I don't gamble! Look,' Sandra felt a desperate need for breathing-space, 'you came here to see Nonie and she's not here at the moment. Why don't you come back later?'

'So you would like me to come back?' he teased.

'Please!' she protested uncomfortably, 'I really must get on.' With relief she recalled certain items of the twins' laundry that needed to be done. About to leave the room, she was forestalled as the back door burst open and the children irrupted through it, stopping short at the sight of the stranger.

After a comprehensive stare, Anna said accusingly, 'You're the man in the Land Rover, the one who was rude to Mummy.'

'I admit it,' Griff said gravely, 'and I assure you I've apologised. Isn't that so, Sandra? Though I'm not sure I'm forgiven.' With a smile like that, Sandra thought hazily, most women would probably forgive him most things short of murder.

'How do you know Mummy's name?'

He crouched down at the child's level, lazily tolerant for a man who had professed only yesterday not to care for children, Sandra mused.

'Your Aunt Nonie told me, before she went down to the shops. She also told me that you're Anna and that your brother is called Leo. Any more questions?'

'Yes, I have a question,' Sandra put in with some indignation. 'I thought you said you hadn't seen Nonie, that you were waiting for her.'

'If you think back you'll recall I didn't say I hadn't seen her. I merely said she wasn't here, which is quite true. She was just on the point of going out when I arrived. She invited me to stay until she got back. She also said I might like to meet you. And when I concluded from her description that Sandra and the twins must be the same delightful trio I'd encountered yesterday, how could I resist?'

'You wanted to see us again?' Anna asked. Grown-ups put things in a strange, complicated way but his underlying meaning was apparent to the intelligent little girl.

'Of course!' he said though his gaze was not on Anna but on her mother and there was an insinuation there Sandra could not ignore. He was implying that he had wanted to see *her* again.

Her heart skipped two or three beats and she wished he wouldn't look at her in that way in front of the twins. Fortunately they were too young to recognise the blatant challenge in his eyes for what it was. She was thankful there was no adult present, whose more perceptive gaze would interpret his openly sexual appraisal. She turned to her son standing quietly at her side. His blue eyes, so like his father's, were summing up the tall man.

'Leo, Aunt Nonie told me you've been exploring the garden.'

'Yes.' His little face glowed with more colour in it than she had seen for some time. 'It's great. It's like a jungle.'

'And we met a stripy cat, just like Granpa's,' Anna contributed. 'It scratched Leo, but,' with evident pride in her brother, 'he didn't cry.'

'Of course not,' Sandra said. Automatically she quoted one of Geoffrey's maxims. 'Big boys don't cry.'

'What rubbish!' The forceful remark came unexpectedly from Griff. 'It's hidebound rules like that which shorten men's lives. Girls and women cry things out of their systems. Boys and men are taught to bottle up their emotions. Consequently they're under stress all their lives.'

Sandra looked at him consideringly. She didn't believe Geoffrey had ever cried in his life, and she couldn't imagine this man shedding tears. Had he ever? The question must have been there in her face, in her eyes, for he said brusquely, 'Yes, if you want to know. I have wept two or three times in my life and I'm not ashamed of it. In the circumstances I'd have been more ashamed of myself if I hadn't shown grief.' He didn't volunteer any more information but Sandra found herself intensely curious as to just what, in Griff's eyes, constituted good cause for grief. But his mood had changed. 'Well now,' he exclaimed, 'here's my favourite girl!'

The back door had opened again and Nonie Hartoch bustled in, with a loaded shopping-basket. Griff moved to take it from her, planting a kiss on her cheek as he did so, and she smiled her thanks.

'So you did stay. And you've met Sandra and the twins. That's nice. Did you offer Griff coffee, dear?' she asked as she began to unload what looked like provisions for a regiment.

'I've had coffee, thanks,' Griff volunteered before Sandra could answer. 'But you look as if you could do with one, Nonie. Sit down.' He shook his coppery head at her in mock reproach. 'I thought the idea of Sandra being here was to give you a break. But you're still dashing here, there and everywhere.' He began to prepare a drink for the elderly woman.

'It's her first day, Griff,' came the gentle reproof. 'Let the poor girl get settled in. And I'll have you know, my lad,' jerking back the wave of iron-grey hair, 'I'm a whole lot tougher than I look. I'm counting on Sandra as company for Amber, not as a general dogsbody.'

'Do you really think Amber and Sandra will have much in common?' There was a note in his voice Sandra did not wholly understand.

'That remains to be seen,' Nonie said repressively, 'and now,' briskly, 'there's work to be done here. What about you, Griff? Aren't you busy up at the Manor?'

'All right! I can take a hint. You want me out of the way. We *are* busy. But that's why I employ a very competent staff.'

'Griff,' Nonie told Sandra with a proprietorial air of pride, 'is our "lord of the manor".'

Was he, Sandra thought with wry amusement. That was a timely warning worth heeding and it would account for much, such as the 'air' she had already noticed. She thought she could understand now his remark that none of his women friends could live up to his life-style. She realised that she had been staring at him and that her thoughts must have been evident in her face. For there was mockery in his tone as he said, 'Sandra doesn't look as impressed by my status as I'd hoped.' And to her, 'I suppose you're not by any chance a socialist or an ardent feminist?'

'Sandra, a feminist?' Nonie said indignantly. 'When you get to know her better, my lad, you'll realise what rubbish that is. She's not one of these hard-boiled career women, but an excellent little wife and mother. The sort of girl I'd hoped to see Dorian marry. Feminist, bah! You'd have shown more perception if you'd said "feminine". It's a great pity you've never met anyone like her.'

'Ah, but I *have* met her now, haven't I, Nonie?' He put an arm about the older woman's shoulders and hugged her. 'And I intend to get to know her better. Which is why,' coaxingly, 'I'm sure you won't keep her tied to your apron strings twenty-four hours a day.'

'Certainly not,' Nonie told him. She seemed much

struck by his remarks, and her glance through steel-rimmed spectacles from Griff to Sandra was speculative. 'Naturally Sandra will have plenty of free time, and I'm sure she'd be delighted for you to take her out sometimes, wouldn't you Sandra?'

Sandra wasn't so certain of that. 'Lords of the manor' with 'life-styles' weren't on her list of desirable male acquaintances. But how to decline politely? She was relieved to have her attention distracted by Leo, who had become bored with this adult conversation.

'Mummy, will you come and see the garden? Anna and I are going to have a secret den.'

'We *were* going to,' Anna put in scathingly, 'until you went and told! Stupid!'

'I'm not stupid,' Leo retorted. 'And we always tell Mummy everything. Daddy was never interested.' Leo's lower lip trembled ominously and Sandra sighed, but before she could intervene,

'I suppose you wouldn't consider showing *me* around?' Griff asked gravely, a hand on Leo's shoulder. 'I used to know this garden pretty well when I was your age.'

There was a long silence as Leo stared up into the tall man's face, and Sandra found that she was holding her breath. Leo made friends very rarely. He seemed particularly nervous of men other than his grandfather.

When Leo finally nodded, a rare smile illuminating his face, she wasn't quite sure whether her relief stemmed from his acceptance of Griff or from the fact that her son had been successfully diverted from the grief that too often overwhelmed him. That extravagant grief puzzled her sometimes. It wasn't as if Geoffrey and his son had been close.

'Can I come too?' Anna demanded.

'Of course.' Griff extended his free hand to her. 'Twins stick together always, don't they?' There was a gentle rebuke implied in his words. But it did not deter Anna from accepting the proffered hand.

'He has a nice manner with them, hasn't he?' Nonie applauded as the trio disappeared into the garden. 'Funny, but I've never known him take such an interest in children before. High time he was married, of course, with some of his own. The Manor needs an heir.'

But Griff had said he wouldn't dream of saddling himself with kids. Sandra remembered his words distinctly. So why was he making overtures to Anna and Leo? Unless . . . unless he was hoping to ingratiate himself with their mother? She felt her cheeks grow warm once more.

Somewhere in the house a bell rang stridently and at once Nonie became agitated.

'Oh dear, that's Amber's bell and her breakfast's not ready.'

'Breakfast?' Sandra raised her eyebrows. It was practically lunch time, which meant the twins would soon be hungry, or at least Anna would. Leo would make some pretence of eating. She must remember to tell Nonie there were only certain things he would eat.

'Do come upstairs and meet her, dear.' Nonie was still fussing. 'Then perhaps I could leave you to help her dress while I prepare a meal. Lunch will have to be a cold one today, for I've no idea when Dorian will be back.'

As Sandra followed Nonie up the steep staircase she wondered how this was going to work out. She had never had any dealings with a fretful invalid. The girl might not take to her. As for herself, she was aware of a certain prejudice against Amber Hartoch. Sandra hoped she wasn't narrow-minded, but she had been brought up to respect the sanctity of her marriage vows. However unhappy she had been with Geoffrey, and there had been times when she had been desperately unhappy, she would never have considered turning to another man. Was Amber unhappy with Dorian? But there was no time for further speculation as Nonie threw open the door of the large bedroom.

'So there you are, Nonie!' It was a petulant cry. 'What does it take to get so much as a cup of tea in this house? I've been awake for hours.'

As Nonie moved ahead of her, Sandra had her first glimpse of Amber Hartoch, of large, extravagantly fringed eyes, a sulky mouth and thick, dark, unruly hair cut in a modern boyish style which gave her a defiant rebellious air. If the other girl were to smile, Sandra thought, she would be very lovely.

'You should have rung before, Amber,' Nonie remonstrated. 'I'm afraid we're rather at sixes and sevens this morning.'

'I thought the idea of having extra people in the house was to help, not hinder.' Now she was closer, Sandra could see that the large eyes were hazel, but unhappy rather than unfriendly.

'And so it will, dear, when we get organised. It's only Sandra's first day. Sandra, this is Amber. I'll leave you two to get acquainted, shall I?'

Warily the two girls took each other's measure.

'I was sorry to hear about your accident,' Sandra ventured. Amber looked pitifully young to be handicapped. The fact that it had probably been her own fault made it no less tragic, she thought, with a little frisson of sympathy for the ruined life. No wonder Amber looked so sullen. The defiant manner was probably a cover for other emotions.

Amber shrugged her acceptance of the remark, but her full-lipped mouth trembled a little. Sandra filled a bowl with hot water from the modern washstand, more of Dorian's industry she guessed, and began to wash the other girl's face and hands.

'What would you like to wear today?' she asked and again Amber shrugged.

'What does it matter, since nobody sees me.'

'What about Dorian?' Sandra said carefully. She must tread warily until she discovered how things lay between husband and wife. 'Surely you want to look nice for him?'

'Dorian sees me when he carries me downstairs and when he brings me back up again.' Sandra had already noticed that the bed was a single one. Bitterly, 'He's more interested in his parishioners than in his wife.'

Had that been the trouble all along? Sandra wondered as she helped the other girl dress.

'I'm afraid there's not a lot more I can do,' Sandra apologised when Amber was seated in the bedside armchair. 'There's no way I can get you downstairs, unless . . .' She was thinking of Griff. Why shouldn't he make himself useful, since he seemed to be so at home about the place? But before she could suggest it,

'You could sit and talk to me. You can't think,' fretfully, 'how boring it is to see the same faces day after day, to hear the same uninteresting conversation. I don't want to know who's died, who's had a baby and whose banns have been called. You've lived in London. Tell me about it. I wish I'd gone to London and got a job instead of getting married and burying myself in this dead-and-alive hole.'

'London can be very lonely too,' Sandra said, hoping she didn't sound as if she were moralising.

'Bright lights don't make up for a lack of loving companionship.' But because she felt really sorry for Amber she went on to talk a little about the city, to describe her life before Geoffrey's death. She told Amber about her parents and about the twins.

'Twins. Yes, Nonie said you had children. I suppose it's them I've heard screaming about the place since some unearthly hour.'

Sandra raised her brows a little at this. The other girl must have very acute hearing, for neither twin was given to noisy play.

'I'm sorry if they disturbed you,' she said a little coolly. Then, 'I'll speak to them, remind them to be quieter first thing in the morning. They've never been used to a garden. I expect they found it all a bit exciting.' Perhaps Amber might resent their presence less when she knew the twins. 'I'll bring them up to see you if you like.

'Don't bother,' Amber drawled. 'I expect I'll see plenty of them when I'm downstairs.'

Sandra felt a sudden impulse to shake her, and reflected that this must be how Nonie felt sometimes. However, she said quietly, 'I take it you're not fond of children.'

'Not especially. Which is probably just as well, seeing I'm never likely to have any of my own.' Was Amber as uncaring as she tried to appear? Sandra wondered doubtfully. Maybe it was a pretence to hide her real feelings.

'I've told you about us. Now it's your turn,' she suggested.

Like Sandra, Amber had been an only child. She spoke affectionately of her mother, now dead. But she had nothing good to say of her father.

'He's a swine! I hate him!' She went on to describe

a tyrannical man, much older than her mother, who had ruled both wife and daughter with martinet-like severity. After her mother's death and until her marriage Amber had felt the full concentration of his will. 'That's one of the reasons I was so glad to get married. It was one way of getting away from *him.*' Amber's was a strong, wilful face. It was surprising, Sandra thought, that her father had been able to rule her so rigidly. But no wonder Amber's marriage hadn't proved successful if her sole motive had been to escape her father's domination.

'How old are you, Amber?'

'Nineteen.' So she had been barely turned seventeen when she had married Dorian Hartoch. And Dorian, Nonie had told Sandra, was now thirty. 'Nineteen,' Amber repeated bitterly, 'and look at me. My life's over.'

'Oh, no!' Sandra exclaimed. She put her hand over one of Amber's. 'Not necessarily. You mustn't give up hope yet. Nonie told me there's still a chance you'll recover the use of your legs.'

'I bet Nonie's told you an awful lot about me.' The hazel eyes were narrowed, but Amber did not shake off Sandra's sympathetic touch. 'I bet you disapprove of me, don't you?'

'It's not my place to judge you,' Sandra said gently. She patted Amber's hand then rose from her chair and moved to the window. From there she could see down into the vast wilderness of the garden, see the twins—and Griff. All three seemed to be enjoying themselves. From this vantage point she could study Griff, acknowledge his attraction without feeling threatened by it.

'I bet your marriage was perfect,' Amber persisted as though she felt compelled to turn the knife in some private wound. 'Rich, successful husband, the statutory two kids, got over with in one fell swoop.'

If only Amber knew, Sandra thought. She turned and met the other's hazel eyes steadily.

'Some day when I know you better, I might tell you about my marriage, Amber. But not today. Right now I think I'd better go and call the twins in and get them cleaned up ready for their lunch. I should think Griff's heartily sick of amusing them by now.'

There was a silence so tangible that she turned to look at the other girl. The sulky face had hardened into palpable dislike.

'Did you say Griff?' Amber asked.

'Yes, why? Do you know him? Oh, I suppose you must. He said he knew you.'

'Is that,' bitterly, 'all he said?'

'Yes, I think so.'

'That figures! I'm surprised he even saw fit to let my name pass his lips. He's an unfeeling, heartless . . .'

Sandra was taken aback. This description didn't seem to fit the man she had met and begun to like. Though to be able to recognise a man's attraction didn't mean he was necessarily an admirable character, she reminded herself. But she found Amber's total condemnation of him rather overdone. No one was all black.

'I gather,' drily, 'that you don't like him, that he's upset you in some way.'

'Upset me!' Amber's normally husky tones had risen to the level of hysteria. 'That has to be the understatement of the year. He's only responsible for ruining my entire life.'

Observing the girl's upset state, the feverish brightness of her eyes, the flushed cheeks, the agitated breathing, Sandra began to put two and two together. Her heart began to beat uncomfortably. Her mouth was suddenly dry. But, oh no, Griff couldn't be . . . She discovered she didn't *want* him to be . . .

'If you know what's good for you,' Amber shrilled, 'you'll steer clear of Griff Faversham.'

'Faversham!' Sandra repeated the name with a sense of dull fatality. So it *was* he. She could hear her mother's voice talking about Amber's accident. 'She got mixed up with some local man called Faversham.' Sandra moved towards the door. She was aware of a burning anger that fought depression for supremacy. 'Excuse me,' she said to Amber. 'But there's something I have to do.'

She ran downstairs and through the kitchen, passing a startled Nonie just on her way to Amber's room with a tastefully arranged tray.

'Oh, Sandra. Since you're here I wonder if you'd . . .'

But, Sandra was already out of the back door and into the jungle-like garden. She found them at the far end. A swing which looked newly constructed had been fastened to a strong bough of an ancient apple tree and Leo, her cautious unadventurous son, was swinging to and fro, higher and higher, pushed by Griff Faversham's hands. Anna meanwhile shrieked encouragement. She turned at Sandra's approach.

'Mummy! Mummy! Uncle Griff's made us a swing. First he pushed me and now he's pushing Leo. He says it would be strong enough for you too. Would you like a go?'

'No, thank you, darling,' Sandra said, amazed that her voice should sound so level. 'I've just come to fetch you in for your lunch.'

'Oh, not yet, Mum!' Leo groaned.

'Yes. *Now,* Leo!' she adjured him sharply. 'Get down please! I want you and Anna to go up to the house at once. Wash your hands and sit up to the table. I'll be with you in a very few minutes.'

'Why? What are you going to do?' Anna asked. 'Are you going to have a swing? Can't we stay and watch?'

'No!' Sandra snapped. She couldn't remember showing impatience with her children before. 'I'm not going to have a swing. I want to talk to Mr Faversham—alone. Now will you please do as I say. Run along.'

She waited tensely, watched as the children slowly and unwillingly disappeared through the overgrown grass and shrubs, waited until they were out of ear-shot. Then she turned to Griff Faversham only to find him close beside her, his vivid green eyes smiling down into hers. She backed away as little sensuous tremors pulsated through her body. She would not be beguiled by his charm.

'You have an extraordinarily expressive face,' he told her. 'Something tells me I'm about to be dealt with as summarily as the twins.'

'I've been talking to Amber,' she said without preamble. She wanted to get this over and get away from him as soon as possible.

'It doesn't seem to have made me any more acceptable to you,' he said perceptively. His eyes were wary now.

'No,' she agreed.

'May I know what she's told you about me?'

'I think you know that.'

'And do I not get a chance to say anything in my own defence?'

'How,' she asked incredulously, 'can you possibly justify what you've done?'

'So, you're on Amber's side?' He sounded disappointed, she thought furiously, as though she were the one at fault. 'Strange. That would have been the last thing I'd have expected of you.'

'I don't take sides,' she told him, 'and I don't hold any brief for Amber or for her behaviour. But you must have known it wouldn't be long before I found out who you were, what you were like.' Indignantly, 'You can't honestly expect me to feel flattered at having been the object of your attentions?'

His face had hardened. So had his eyes.

'My attentions, as you call them, were a genuine expression of my admiration for you, of my wish to get to know you better. And I thought you realised that. But now you seem to regard them as an insult. I wish I knew why.'

Sandra gasped in outrage. To stand there and pretend he didn't know! And how on earth, she wondered, had he the nerve to visit this house, to make himself so utterly at home under Dorian's roof? What was Nonie thinking of to make him welcome, and actually to encourage the invitation he had extended to herself?

'Mr Faversham,' she drew herself up to her five foot five inches, 'I shouldn't have to explain to you. If you had the sensitivity of soul you claim to have you'd know you shouldn't be here. You should know why I can't have anything to do with you.'

As she spoke his eyes had narrowed and now he moved towards her, grasped her by the shoulders. But there was nothing flirtatious or caressive in the gesture this time.

Sandra swallowed convulsively, closing her eyes and her mind against the anger and more than anger she sensed in him. There was pain, but more than pain in her as he held her scarcely a half-inch from his hard body.

'Nevertheless,' he said grimly, 'I think I'd better know exactly what Amber Hartoch has been saying about me.'

'All right!' Sandra threw her head back, arching the lovely line of her throat at him. Eyes, grey ice now, condemned him. 'I've just found out that you were the one responsible for her accident. That it's thanks to you a nineteen-year-old girl is condemned to spend the rest of her life in a wheelchair!'

He released her as though his hands had been scorched by her anger. His expression bleak, he uttered only the words 'I see', then he turned on his heel and strode away from her.

Sandra watched him go. She stood there, long after he was out of sight, fighting back an odd feeling of desolation. What had she expected? That he would deny it? How could he when he was guilty? Thank God she had found out in time just who he was and what he had done.

CHAPTER THREE

'GRIFF gone?' Nonie was setting sausages and chips before the twins. That was a relief. They were Leo's staple diet.

'Yes, he's gone.' Sandra said it so tautly that Nonie looked sharply at her.

'Why, whatever's the matter, dear? You look as though you'd seen a ghost.'

The door opening behind her spared Sandra the necessity of replying. She would have to broach the subject of Griff Faversham with Nonie some time, but she didn't want to rush into speech until she had regained control of herself. She was still angry, angrier than she could ever remember feeling. It was an anger that made her feel weak and shaky. But most of all she was confused by her own reactions. She was still pulled by his attraction even though she was repelled by the knowledge of who he was and what he had done.

'Dorian!' Nonie exclaimed with pleasure. 'At last!'

So this was Nonie's beloved nephew. He didn't look any more like a clergyman than Griff had, was Sandra's first thought. He was dressed in old slacks and a bright blue shirt that emphasised the brilliant colour of his eyes. He was of medium height, slightly but wirily built. She forced a smile to her face and put her hand into his.

'Hello,' he greeted her. 'You must be Sandra.' He sank into a chair at the head of the table with a sigh that was clearly one of tired relief. 'Gosh, it's been a long night.' His triangular face beneath a shock of dark untidy hair was weary. There were dark rings under the blue eyes. His chin was unshaven. But despite fatigue his mouth was good humoured, its pleasant line accentuated by a small moustache.

'He's passed over then?' Nonie asked.

'Yes.' He looked at his watch. 'Goodness!' He sprang to his feet again. 'I didn't realise it was that late. I'd better bring Amber down.'

'You stay where you are and get this inside you first!' Nonie pressed him back into his seat and put a loaded plate before him. 'Amber's only just this moment got her brunch. It won't do her any harm to wait a while longer.'

'Have you met my wife yet?' Dorian asked Sandra, and as she nodded, 'I hope you'll be able to cheer her up. Poor girl, I'm afraid it's not much of an existence for her these days.'

'She brought it on herself,' his aunt pointed out rather sharply, and Dorian sighed and shook his head.

'I don't like to hear you speak that way, Nonie. It's not like you to be uncharitable.'

'Uncharitable! Me!' Nonie banged a vegetable dish down on the table, then encountered Leo's apprehensive stare, and looked from him to Anna's unwinking fascinated gaze. 'This isn't the time or the place to discuss it,' she said shortly.

The meal was eaten in a tacit but uneasy silence until the twins asked permission to leave the table. Then Nonie laid down her knife and fork and pushed away her almost untouched plate, and ran a trembling hand through the iron-grey bob of her hair.

'It's no good, Dorian. I can't go on bottling it up! I've got to say it or I shall burst!'

Feeling distinctly embarrassed, Sandra half rose.

'I'll go and . . .'

'No, Sandra!' Nonie held out a restraining hand. 'You're going to be living here in the middle of all this. It's only fair you should know the rights and wrongs of it.'

'Nonie, please!' Dorian was on his feet. He hadn't made a very good meal either.

'I know what you're going to say,' Nonie told him, ' "Judge not that ye be not judged." But you of all people can't tell me marriage vows aren't to be observed. How can I stand by and see what Amber's done to you, is still doing to you, and say nothing? Am I supposed to forget what . . .?'

'Forget?' Dorian repeated the word harshly. He began to pace the room, one hand further dishevelling his unruly hair. 'Do you think *I* can forget? But I can, *must* try to forgive, to understand. If I don't, what am I? What kind of clergyman, if I can't practise what I preach?' His pleasant face was twisted with anguish. Sandra felt pity well within her. Not only Amber but Griff Faversham was responsible for this man's torture, and yet somehow she had liked both of them. Her judgement must be sadly at fault somewhere.

'I wouldn't mind so much,' Nonie continued, 'if only Amber had ever shown the slightest sign of repentance. But she hasn't. The only person she's sorry for is herself.'

'Understandable, surely?' Dorian's tone was wry.

'But she ought to be sorry for hurting *you,* for making a mockery of your marriage in front of your parishioners. There isn't one of them doesn't know she was running around with another man.'

Dorian turned to Sandra, blue eyes apologetic. 'I'm sorry. You must be wondering what kind of household you've come to.'

'No,' she said quickly, earnestly. 'I understand. All

families have their problems and of course it's none of my business. But what I don't understand is why you haven't mentioned the other culprit in this affair. Why you seem to be able to forget and presumably forgive what *he's* done. He still seems to come and go here as he pleases. Nonie treats him like one of the family.' She looked from one to the other in bewilderment. 'It just doesn't make sense.'

'My dear child,' Nonie exclaimed, adjusting steel-rimmed spectacles, 'whatever are you talking about?'

'Griff Faversham! He doesn't seem the least bit concerned about . . .'

'Griff?' Dorian queried. 'But Griff's done nothing to be ashamed of. I sometimes think he's the only one to come out of this affair with any credit at all.'

'What?' Sandra couldn't believe her ears. 'He has an affair with your wife, nearly gets her killed and . . .'

'Wherever did you . . .? Oh, I see.' Enlightenment came to Nonie. 'My dear, it wasn't *Griff* Faversham that Amber was seeing. It was his younger brother, Gerald. Gerald was killed in the accident that crippled Amber. Griff has always been welcome here. He's a very good friend of ours and so is his mother.' Nonie sighed. 'Poor Molly Faversham's never been very robust, and since the accident I've seen a real deterioration in her. Why, Sandra, whatever is it?'

For at Nonie's words Sandra's hands had flown to her cheeks. Her eyes had widened with horror.

'Oh, no! Oh, how awful! Oh, Nonie, I said the most dreadful things to him. I didn't know until Amber told me that his name was Faversham and then she seemed so bitter towards him, I naturally assumed . . .' She realised she was growing incoherent. 'What have I done?'

'Poor Griff!' Nonie could manage a wry smile at the

irony of it. 'If anyone was undeserving of censure . . . He did his best to put a stop to his brother's shenanigans. Gerald was a lot younger than Griff, closer to Amber in age. Griff had been almost a father to him since their own died. And though the lad was wild, Griff was fond of him. It was a dreadful shock to him, and a great grief, when Gerald was killed like that.'

This was only making Sandra feel worse. In fact she felt quite sick. Now she too pushed her unfinished meal away from her. There was going to be a great deal of wasted food today.

'Don't worry, dear,' Nonie said, observing her stricken face and gesture of repulsion. 'I'm sure Griff will understand when you explain.'

Explain! Yes, she'd have to do that of course, and she'd have to apologise to him. The very thought made Sandra quiver inside. The thought of having to face those mocking green eyes. But they might not be mocking. They might be cold, angry, and it would be no more than she deserved for jumping to conclusions.

'But about Amber, Dorian.' Nonie's thoughts had reverted to her earlier topic.

'No, Nonie!' Dorian said. 'No more. It's a profitless subject. What's done is done and will just have to be endured, by us as well as by her. I'll go and fetch her down.'

'I worry about Dorian,' Nonie told Sandra as the door closed behind her nephew. 'He's beginning to look very fine-drawn. He works so hard, in the parish and here at home. To begin with he was happy. I think if one's happy one can put up with any amount of hard work. He should have married a girl who'd be a help to him.'

'He's always got you,' Sandra reminded her gently.

But she felt concerned for Nonie. She didn't like to see the older woman looking so distressed. At seventy-odd it couldn't be good for her to have so much work and worry.

'Yes, but I'm slowing down,' Nonie confessed ruefully, displaying her arthritic hands. 'Sandra dear, whilst you're here would you spend some of your time helping Dorian? He needs somebody young and energetic to do his running around for him.'

'But what about Amber? I thought I . . .?'

'Some of the time, yes. But as far as I'm concerned Dorian's welfare is more important. I don't want him to make himself ill.'

'I'll do whatever I can, of course,' Sandra promised. 'I'll be glad to, though I've no experience of parish work.' Their discussion ended as Dorian returned, carrying Amber in his arms, and set her down in one of the fireside chairs.

'Are you going to catch up on some sleep now?' Nonie asked him, but he shook his head.

'Can't. I've got a man coming this morning to look at the church roof. There seems to be a damp patch developing on the wall behind St Thomas's altar. Then I want to look at that wretched churchyard. Something's got to be done and soon.'

'You'll kill yourself, Dorian,' Nonie worried. Then with sudden inspiration, 'Sandra dear, you looked quite pale for a few minutes just now. You could do with some fresh air. Go along with Dorian and keep an eye on him for me—see he doesn't overdo things.'

'Meanwhile, I suppose,' Amber put in sulkily, 'I sit here and watch you being domesticated—doing all the things I ought to do.'

'Perhaps I should stay with Amber,' Sandra suggested hastily, foreseeing more domestic squalls.

'Or do some baking for you. I know nothing at all about church roofs.'

'But I believe you know something about landscaping,' Dorian said. 'Isn't your father a landscape gardener?' and as Sandra nodded, 'Did any of his expertise rub off on you?'

'I used to help him, in the holidays, before I got married.'

'Well then, come and give me the benefit of your advice. I don't mind work once I know where to start. Nonie's a dab hand at interior decorating, but she's not into gardening.'

Sandra looked from face to face. She was torn between a very real desire to help this nice young man and the fact that her initial brief had been to cope with Amber. It was Amber who settled the matter.

'It's quite obvious,' she said sarcastically, 'that Dorian's need is greater than mine. Do go with him, Sandra.' Ostentatiously she opened a glossy magazine she had been holding and immersed herself in its pages.

Oddly, Sandra felt that Amber would have liked her to stay. But Nonie was watching her expectantly, Dorian was patiently waiting and Amber refused to look up. Shrugging her shoulders, Sandra turned and followed Dorian out into the garden and through the private gate which opened into the churchyard.

The church, Dorian said, had been built in the thirteenth century, but had been so frequently restored and altered that it was a hotch-potch of architectural styles.

'Which gives it a rather unique appearance, but it isn't exactly beautiful,' he added wryly, 'which is why I aim to improve its surroundings at least. Young couples don't want to get married here. They say it doesn't look well on the wedding photos! They'd rather go into the nearest town, to the register office. And that doesn't look good from where I stand. I thought perhaps some kind of rockery, and a rose bower.'

'Can't you get some of your parishioners to muck in and help with the heavy work?' Sandra asked as she surveyed the rough overgrown terrain.

Dorian spread his hands in a gesture of resignation.

'Those that would be willing are too old. Those fit enough aren't interested. Besides,' cheerfully, 'God helps those who help themselves.'

That was all very well, Sandra reflected. But would the sight of Dorian wielding pickaxe and spade move God to send in volunteers? Then she decided it might be best not to voice such doubts to a clergyman. Besides, Dorian seemed to think God had already provided.

'After all, I've got you now, to help with Amber and to advise me on this lot. That's more than I had last week,' he concluded.

'I suppose it would cost you too much to have it done professionally,' she suggested as they moved on.

''Fraid so. In such a small parish fund-raising events don't amount to much. The Church Commissioners paid for the removal of the old tombstones. They've been incorporated in the churchyard wall. These days burials are conducted around the back. So I can do what I like with this patch, but it's all down to my own resources.'

The builder's man had not arrived and they filled in time by looking around the church itself.

'We've tried to brighten it up a bit.' Dorian pointed to flower arrangements, brightly coloured banners and tapestry-covered kneelers. 'Made by Nonie's

Ladies' Circle. A formidable bunch, and I rather suspect a lot of gossiping goes on as well as needlework.'

'Never mind! At least uncharitableness has covered a multitude of hassocks!' Sandra's delightful laugh rang through the old building, and after a moment Dorian joined in. Crease lines at his eyes and mouth had suggested he had a well developed sense of humour, but she suspected Dorian didn't laugh very often these days. It was good to see his strained face relax into a grin.

'Oh, Sandra!' He flung a friendly arm about her shoulders and hugged her. 'Just lately things have been getting us down, all of us. But I think you're going to be good for us!'

'I hope so,' she said, meeting his gaze earnestly. 'And I think being here is going to help me too.'

It was only the slightest sound that attracted Sandra's attention, and made her look beyond Dorian's shoulder, where she met the cold, direct gaze of Griff Faversham, before he swung away and left the church as silently as he had entered it. How long had he been there? Dorian, she was sure, had noticed nothing, and she wondered whether she should mention Griff's brief appearance, but then the builder's man arrived and they followed him on his tour of inspection.

The next few days passed fairly quietly. There were crises, but only minor domestic ones such as a spat between the twins who were now enrolled in the small modern school at Filberton some ten miles from Vicar's Oak. There were more displays of petulance from Amber. But there were no more visits from Griff Faversham, and Sandra wasn't sure whether her sense of anticlimax was based on relief or disappointment that there was no opportunity of explaining, of apologising to him.

Thursday afternoons, Nonie informed Sandra, were sacrosanct to her Ladies' Sewing Circle.

'Perhaps you'd like to join us, dear? It would be an opportunity for you to get to meet people.'

'Do you go, Amber?' Sandra asked. She had made determined efforts to get to know Dorian's wife, curbing her natural impatience with Amber's more unreasonable moods, and once or twice she had thought she might be breaking through the younger woman's hostile front. Beneath the sulky indifference, the don't-care attitude, Sandra thought she sensed a very unhappy girl, perhaps even a much nicer person than anyone else suspected. Was it that nicer person with whom Dorian had fallen in love, had continued to love until everything had gone so disastrously wrong? Why had it gone wrong, when Dorian seemed to be such a good, caring man?

'I'm afraid Amber doesn't like sewing,' Nonie put in, with more truth than tact, Sandra thought.

'Or the members of your precious circle,' Amber put in with a toss of her boyish dark head. 'Nosy, gossiping old trouts.'

'They're not all old.' Nonie was tart. 'Some of them are people who might have been your friends. And if you mean they gossip about you, it's only what you've given them cause for.'

Amber chose not to answer and Sandra hastily changed the subject, but once again she thought she glimpsed a desperate misery in the other's large hazel eyes.

Sandra entered the parlour on that first Thursday afternoon not quite knowing what to expect. She was pleasantly surprised. As Nonie had said, the women came from a wide age range. Grandmothers sat side by side with and conversed with young mothers. The current project was not sewing this time but knitting colourful woollen vests for underprivileged African children. Most women had brought their own wool and needles. Nonie dispensed coffee and biscuits and moved from group to group organising and encouraging, but so unobtrusively that Sandra had to admire her tactics. Amber, she reflected, could have learned much from Nonie, had she been willing to do so.

Among those present was Mrs Faversham, who looked too ridiculously tiny and frail to be Griff's mother. At first Sandra felt horribly self-conscious as she wondered if the elderly lady had heard an account of Sandra's behaviour towards her son. But Mrs Faversham was charming to her in a vague, somewhat distraite manner.

'I understand from Nonie that you have twins, one of them a boy. Sons can be such a delight, but such a worry too.' Her lined face contorted in a sudden spasm of pain and Sandra guessed she was thinking of the son she had lost. Diffidently, she expressed her sympathy. Whatever the rights or wrongs of the case, whether or not Gerald Faversham had been a bad-hat, to Mrs Faversham he had been a dearly loved child.

'Thank you, my dear.' The small elderly woman laid a hand on Sandra's. 'You can't know what an inexpressible relief it is to be able to talk about him. So many people avoid the subject. Perhaps they're afraid I shall lose control in front of them and embarrass them.' She went on with a trace of bitterness. 'Though I suspect some don't speak of him because they disapproved of his behaviour, the circumstances in which he died. And the vicar, poor man,' Mrs Faversham said of Dorian. 'However can he bear to think of his wife's part in it?' She leant forward confidentially. 'I flatter myself I'm a good judge of character. The dear Vicar should have married someone like you. A nice, steady, domesticated girl. I'm not in favour of divorce and I suppose it would be quite unthinkable for a member of the clergy. But sometimes I feel he would be better off without that wife of his.'

Before she left Mrs Faversham made a special point of bidding Sandra goodbye and of issuing an invitation.

'It would please me so much, my dear, if you could spare the time to come up to the Manor and see me sometimes. Will you come? Or do you consider me to be a maudlin old nuisance?'

'You're not anything of the sort. Of course I'll come.' Sandra spoke impulsively out of the depths of her compassion, then realised too late what she had done.

She liked Mrs Faversham, pitied her distress, understood her need to unburden herself to sympathetic ears. But the Manor was Griff's home too and he wasn't on speaking terms with her. 'That is,' she faltered, 'if you don't think your son would mind . . . your elder son.' Now was the time for Mrs Faversham to reveal if Griff had spoken of her.

'Why on earth should he mind?' Mrs Faversham was astonished at the idea. 'Besides, he's at the house very little. The estate keeps him very busy, that and his pet project.'

Sandra wondered very much just what Griff Faversham's 'pet project' might be, but just then Nonie bustled over to bid Mrs Faversham goodbye and there was no opportunity for questions. This was just as well perhaps, she thought afterwards. She didn't want it getting back to Griff that she was showing interest in him and his pursuits, not when her manner towards him must have destroyed all *his* interest in *her*. The thought made her feel oddly despondent.

'Molly Faversham tells me she's invited you up to the Manor,' Nonie said when she came back from seeing the other woman out. 'That's quite a compliment, Sandra dear. With her poor health she doesn't issue many invitations. You'll go of course.' It was a statement, not a question.

'I'd like to,' Sandra said, 'but . . .' She explained her misgivings.

'Nonsense, dear. I've known Griff Faversham for ages and there's not an ounce of malice in the man. And besides, he quite obviously took a liking to you. If you meet him, and you're bound to sooner or later anyway, just take your courage in both hands and explain the misunderstanding to him.'

Despite Nonie's advice it was the following Monday before Sandra plucked up the nerve to telephone the Manor and ask if she might visit Mrs Faversham that afternoon. She kept her fingers crossed that Griff wouldn't answer the phone himself. But of course she should have known there would be servants. A staid-sounding man asked her to hold on, stating that he would enquire whether Madam was receiving today. When he returned, however, his manner was much less formal and his message was that Mrs Faversham would be delighted to see Mrs Tyler at two-thirty if that was convenient, and would she please stay for tea.

Sandra felt she could hardly refuse, but after she had put the phone down she began to worry about the twins coming in from school and not finding her there.

'My dear,' Nonie said, 'you must be the most conscientious mother living! But you can't devote every single moment of your time to the twins. They'll be perfectly all right with me. You go and enjoy yourself. Molly Faversham's house is a delightful old place, and though she's very frail these days she'll still insist on showing you round and telling you the family history. You'll love every moment of it.'

Sandra hesitated over what she should wear for her afternoon engagement. The Favershams, mother and son, had only seen her in serviceable but unglamorous jeans. But the fact that she might encounter Griff had no bearing on what she wore, she assured herself firmly.

The dress she finally chose was a crisp cotton in a rose-pink that lent an added glow to her cheeks, and she knew as she surveyed herself in the bedroom mirror that its tightly cinched waist and flared skirt emphasised her slim figure. Looking at her, no one would ever guess, she thought a little complacently, that she was the mother of two children. Her hips were as neat, her stomach as flat as they had been before she had married Geoffrey.

It was a fine day and she decided to walk up to the Manor House. The winding lane from the village seemed to have gathered and held all the warmth of the sunny day. The lane ran alongside a sloping orchard that rose up a hillside to her left and ended at the gate of the superbly situated Manor House. Early sixteenth century with great chimneys and crow-stepped gables, it stood in the shelter of rising ground on north, east and west, with a view south across the Weald.

The staid man of her telephone conversation proved to be the archetypal butler. He showed her into a gold and ochre drawing-room, the elegance of which made Sandra draw in her breath. Geoffrey had had some wealthy friends, but none of them had lived in such state. Pale gold damask covered the walls, matching the elaborately swagged and tasselled curtains. There were no carpets. Instead costly rugs islanded a wooden floor that gleamed like gold. From one of a pair of Chippendale sofas covered in yellow silk, Mrs Faversham rose to greet her.

'Sandra, my dear—I may call you Sandra? Thank you so much for keeping your promise. Now, I'm sure you must be thirsty after that walk up from the village. So Meredith will serve us a nice cup of tea in here and then, if you won't find it too boring, I shall show you around my dear old house.'

It was far from boring. But it was a little daunting. As Sandra followed Molly Faversham through the lofty rooms, she marvelled that anyone could ever live familiarly with so much magnificence. Here Mrs Faversham displayed a cabinet of Sèvres china, there an Old Master. Coming suddenly upon a full-length portrait in one of the rooms made Sandra start nervously. It was so lifelike. Griff could have posed for it, if the clothes had not been those of the previous generation. There was that same not-quite-handsome face, the widely spaced green eyes, the long sensual mouth that seemed to be laughing at her just as Griff's had done. The hair, though shorter than was worn by present-day men, had the same coppery sheen.

'My late husband as a young man,' Mrs Faversham said fondly. 'I adored him. You can see why, can't you? My elder son takes after him. Gerald,' she sighed, 'was more like my side of the family, a smaller, slighter build, fair haired.'

The grounds too had their wonders, including an

Elizabethan parterre with hedges of clipped box and a secluded rose-garden. But best of all Sandra liked the walled garden with its fruit trees, from which the last of the spring blossom was still suspended. Narrow paths threaded through beds of scarlet tulips, startling explosions of colour among clouds of blue forget-me-nots. Over everything drifted the scent of aromatic plants. And here the two women discovered a common bond.

'This is the only place where I'm allowed to potter,' Molly Faversham said. 'Since I had my heart attack my doctor has forbidden all but a little gentle weeding. I've always loved gardening.'

'Me too.' Sandra told the older woman about her father's landscape-gardening business, which to him was not just a job but a constant source of pleasure. She spoke also of Dorian's ideas for improving the frontage of his church.

Back then to the mellow-bricked house where a trim maid this time served wafer-thin cucumber sandwishes and melt-in-the-mouth fancy cakes. Home baked, Molly Faversham told Sandra with quiet pride.

'I insist on being allowed to use my own kitchen occasionally. Of course I'm very fortunate in having such an excellent family working for me. Meredith's wife is the cook. Their daughter, Susan Bradshaw—she's married to our farm manager—keeps house and supervises the daily women. And the child who brought the tea in is the Merediths' granddaughter.'

After tea, Mrs Faversham sighed wistfully.

'I do wish I could keep you a little longer, for the evening, for dinner. I'd like you to meet Griff.'

'Actually,' Sandra felt bound to confess, 'I have met your elder son.'

'Really? I'd no idea! The naughty boy! He never said a word to me. This was at Dorian's, I suppose?'

At this point the stately Meredith entered once again to announce that Madam was wanted on the telephone by a Mrs Carstairs. Mrs Faversham's nose wrinkled ruefully.

'That means a good half-hour session. Dear Deborah! Such a chatterbox! Well, Sandra, it seems our lovely visit is over after all. My dear, before you go home, do go back to my kitchen garden and pick some flowers for Nonie.'

Sandra felt a little diffident about this commission, but Mrs Faversham insisted.

The sun was low in the sky as she re-entered the walled garden but the enclosed space seemed to have trapped and held its warmth. As she picked the tulips her fingers brushed against the herbs, the scent of thyme and mint heavy in her nostrils. How she would love a garden like this, a quiet, secret, reposeful place, where time seemed suspended beneath a sensuous enchanter's spell.

Alerted by a vigilant gardener to the fact that a stranger was wandering around the grounds and had last been seen entering the kitchen garden, Griff Faversham made his way in that direction.

He rounded a corner. At first, with the gaudiness of the sinking sun in his eyes, he saw no one. Then a blur of colour resolved itself into the figure of a woman. Dressed in glowing pink, she stood against a background of verdant greens and snowy blossoms. Around her feet a haze of blue gave an impression of disembodiment. She was moving towards him, her head down-bent over the blazing scarlet flowers she held. In the brown hair veiling her face the sun lit golden lights, and for a brief incredulous moment, Griff thought he was seeing a vision. Then, as if suddenly aware of his presence, she lifted her head and he witnessed the gamut of emotions that crossed the pure oval of her face. He saw the lovely colour run up into her cheeks, the grey eyes widen, saw her breast rise and fall on a startled inhalation of breath.

At their first encounter, Sandra thought, with an odd little lunge of her heart, she had been quite positive that Griff Faversham was not a handsome man. So why ever since had she found herself responding so disastrously to the sight of him, to his physical presence?

'What on earth are you doing here?' he demanded.

'I've been having tea with your mother,' she told him, a little breathlessly. 'She asked me to pick some flowers to take back for Nonie.'

'Tea? With my mother?' He sounded incredulous. 'How did that come about?' Then his face hardened and he took a step towards her. 'And what sort of things have you been saying to my mother over the teacups? If you've said anything to upset her . . .'

'Of course I haven't!' Sandra said with some heat. She rushed into speech as impulsively as her mother might have done. 'I know what you're thinking. About what I said to you. But that was a dreadful mistake. Nonie told me about your brother and I've been wanting to apologise ever since.'

'Is that why you're here?' He looked even more fierce, if that were possible. 'Good God, you haven't told my mother that you thought I . . .?'

'No!' Sandra snapped, indignant that he should think her capable of such a *faux pas*. 'I met your mother at the vicarage and she invited me to visit her. I agreed because I liked her very much, certainly not to talk about you or because I thought I might see you,' she assured him.

'In fact you hoped you wouldn't?' he finished wryly, but his face had relaxed a little.

'I didn't say that,' she protested. 'I'd made up my mind to explain to you, to apologise, if and when we met.'

'And if we hadn't?'

'I would have written a note.'

'But now we have met.' Moving even closer now, he lifted sardonically enquiring brows at her and she realised he wasn't going to be satisfied with a mere statement of intent. He wanted his pound of flesh. He was standing so close to her she could sense the strength of him and it seemed to her that tension quivered between them. Sandra's fingers tightened their grip upon the flowers, endangering their fragile stems. She took a deep breath, steadying herself.

'All right.' She managed to meet his eyes squarely, even though something enigmatic in their green depths was still causing her this shattering inner turmoil. 'Mr Faversham, I apologise. When I said what I did, I thought you were the Faversham whose name I'd heard in connection with Amber. It was an understandable mistake, surely?' she finished, abandoning formality on a defensive note.

'Understandable? Why? In what way?' Not only his pound of flesh! He seemed determined to draw every ounce out of the situation. But Sandra was beginning to feel that she had eaten humble pie long enough, and anyway indignation was a better defence against this dizzying current of chemical attraction.

'Understandable because I couldn't know you had a brother.'

'And now that you know about Gerald?'

'I've said I'm sorry,' she reminded him sharply. His attitude puzzled her. 'What more do you want?'

'I don't know,' he muttered. 'I suppose I want to know just whose side you're on. When you thought I was the culprit you seemed to be taking Amber Hartoch's part.'

'I told you then,' Sandra reminded him firmly, 'I don't take sides.' Then her voice gentled as she almost pleaded with him for understanding. 'But I can't help feeling sorry for her. She's so young to be crippled. I'm sorry for everyone involved—for Nonie, for Dorian . . .'

'For Dorian? Yes!' Without him telling her, she knew he was thinking of the scene he had witnessed in the church. She was worried that he had read something into it that didn't exist. But if she referred to the incident, tried to explain away the innocent episode, it made too much of it. 'Just how sorry for Dorian are you?' he asked, confirming her supposition.

'As sorry as I'd be for anyone in similar circumstances,' she said repressively. 'And now I have to go. I'm later than I said I'd be.' She looked beyond him, at the narrow path he was still blocking. He made no attempt to move out of her way, and the totally irrational thought that he might physically prevent her from leaving brought a throb of sensation to the pit of her stomach.

'But we have a truce, do we?' he asked.

Sandra wasn't sure what they had now.

'Oh, come on, Sandra.' He resolved the matter for her. 'It's obvious we'll never agree on the subject of Amber Hartoch. So I suppose we'll have to agree to differ.' He held out a large long-fingered hand towards her. 'Shall we shake on it?' he suggested.

'All right.' Relief flooded through her. She didn't

want to be at odds with Griff Faversham. Her mouth, unconsciously wistful in repose, curved into a smile, dazzling in the way in which it transformed her grave little face. She put her slender fingers into his, felt them engulfed. His grasp tightened over hers and the pull of his hand drew her a little nearer to him. Her heart began to thump and she couldn't repress a swift, startled upward look, found his eyes enigmatic and guarded. She thought for a moment that he intended to seal their bargain not only with a handshake but with a kiss, and the thought sent little sensuous tremors pulsating through her body. But after a long moment in which his green eyes seemed to search her face he nodded as though reaching some decision, then released her hand and stood aside. The moment was shattered, the promise it had seemed to hold unfulfilled. She was aware of a tremendous sense of anticlimax.

'Would you like me to run you back to the vicarage?' he asked. He was walking close behind her, and her senses still tingled at his proximity.

'No, thank you.' The thought of being confined with him in his car was far too disturbing. 'I enjoy walking.' Besides, before she was thrown back into the domestic situations of the vicarage, surrounded by other people and their needs, she wanted some time to herself, to think. She wasn't quite sure what she had expected to happen once Griff had accepted her apology. But his handshake had seemed a prosaic way to end their encounter and she still felt oddly deflated. Of course there was no reason why he should have attempted to kiss her. She hadn't *wanted* him to kiss her, she told herself, and yet . . .

'Very well! Then I'll walk with you. I enjoy walking too.'

They set off in silence. For the life of her Sandra couldn't think of anything to say.

'How are the twins settling down?' Griff asked at last, and she had an almost intuitive feeling that this subject wasn't the one uppermost in his mind, but introduced as some kind of preliminary. He had set the pace of their walk and seemed to be in no hurry. Except for her unease, they might have been friends of long standing taking a leisurely ramble together.

'Very well. Better than I expected. They like Vicar's Oak and they seem happy at their new school.'

'They're as alike as two peas to look at, but they're very different in temperament,' Griff observed shrewdly. 'Young Leo seems the nervy, highly strung type.'

'He's always been sensitive.' This worry was never far from Sandra and a frown furrowed her brow. 'But he's been worse since he lost his father.'

'And he seems to cling to you. Perhaps he's afraid you're going to put some other man in his father's place.' It was lightly said and yet seemed to require an answer.

Sandra laughed aloud in genuine amusement.

'Is the idea so ridiculous?' Griff asked more sharply, she thought, than the occasion warranted.

'No. That is . . . It's just that I shouldn't think the idea's even crossed his mind,' she explained. 'He's only seven. Anyway,' more soberly, 'he and Geoffrey didn't hit it off. Geoffrey didn't like children.'

But apparently Griff wasn't interested in Geoffrey's likes and dislikes.

'But you don't discount the idea of marrying again?'

'Not altogether. But I've only been widowed two months and as I haven't met anyone yet who . . .' The words trailed away as Griff put a hand under her elbow to steer her across the suddenly busy road. 'Anyway,' she went on hurriedly, 'even if I did I'd be much more wary this time. I won't allow myself to be rushed into anything.'

'You were rushed into marriage before?' he asked curiously. 'Why was that?'

'Because I was very much in love,' she hastened to explain in case he should fall into a misconception. 'I *wanted* to get married. It was an *emotional* decision.'

'I gather from your tone of voice that next time you'll be ruled by your head. By other considerations.'

'Yes!' Sandra was very positive.

'Such as?' he wanted to know.

'Oh . . .' Sandra didn't want to go into the unsatisfactory aspects of her first marriage. 'The kind of life the man leads, his profession or position in life. That sort of thing can make all the difference to a woman's happiness. At least it can to mine.'

'I see!' Griff sounded vaguely disapproving. 'Thank you for visiting my mother,' he said rather formally as they reached the vicarage. 'She doesn't go out as much as she used to. I'm afraid she's not very strong. In fact I've been trying to persuade her to take a cruise, to recuperate.'

'Visiting her was a pleasure for *me,*' Sandra said warmly. 'I like her.' Then, 'Won't you come in—to see Nonie?' she added hastily. But she knew it was because she was suddenly reluctant to part from him.

'I think not.' He raised his hand in a casual half-salute. 'Goodbye, Sandra.'

He hadn't even waited to see her enter the house, she thought ruefully, as he turned on his heel and strode away. Nor had he mentioned any possibility of their meeting again.

'For goodness' sake,' she admonished herself aloud as she walked briskly up the path to the house. 'Why ever should he want to see any more of you?'

CHAPTER FOUR

IT was customary for members of the vicarage household—as well as close friends—to use the back door, and this Sandra did, pausing on the threshold in amazement at the scene before her, at hearing the sound of delighted giggling.

There was no sign of Nonie. The twins, perched one on either arm of the large chair, were absorbed in something its occupant was telling them. Sandra scarcely recognised Amber. Her normally sullen face was alight with laughter. She looked scarcely any older than the twins at that moment. But then, Sandra thought, she was little more than a child, a child who, by all accounts, had led an oppressed life. There couldn't have been much laughter in Amber's childhood.

As Sandra closed the door behind her, all three looked up and Amber's face once more became closed in and defensive. Anna ran to Sandra, offering her face up for a kiss. But it was Leo, still seated at Amber's side, who said,

'Hallo Mummy! Auntie Amber's been telling us about when she was a little girl.'

'Aunt Nonie had to go out,' Anna said, then, importantly, 'she said *we* had to look after Auntie Amber. We helped Auntie Amber make our supper.'

'Make the supper? But . . .' Sandra's heart lurched. Suppose there had been some crisis, a fire perhaps. How were seven-year-old children supposed to cope with that *and* an invalid woman? It would have been tactless to put her thoughts into words but as always her face betrayed her feeling, for,

'It's all right,' Sandra!' Amber spoke impatiently. 'Don't flap. Dorian's in the house too. He's in his study preparing his sermon for next Sunday.'

Sandra relaxed. It was all very well to say 'don't flap'. But until you had had children you didn't realise half the worries. Or the joys, she reminded herself penitently. Poor Amber might never know either.

'Say goodnight and thank you to Auntie Amber now, twins,' Sandra told them. 'Bath and bedtime!' An order which did not meet with their approval. They wanted, they protested in unison, more stories from Amber.

'Tomorrow,' Amber volunteered, surprising Sandra. She lingered a little behind the departing twins to lift her eyebrows at Dorian's wife in comical enquiry.

'They're not half bad, your kids.' Amber was off-hand but Sandra felt her manner was assumed. 'Better company than Nonie.'

'You don't like Nonie very much, do you?' Sandra said. 'Why? What's she ever done to you?'

'By *her* lights?' Amber shrugged. 'Nothing, I suppose. I don't actually dislike her. But sometimes I wish . . .'

'Yes?'

'Oh, nothing! No,' as Sandra lingered expectantly, 'you wouldn't understand.'

'You could try me some time,' Sandra suggested, but she did not press the point just then. Maybe in time Amber would trust her sufficiently to be more explicit.

* * *

A day or two later after dropping the twins at school in Filberton, Sandra called on Crosthwaites, a firm of landscape gardeners. She wanted some professional advice about the landscaping of the churchyard. She could have consulted her father, but his firm was too far distant. Transport costs and accommodation for labourers would have made a quotation from him uneconomic.

Though Dorian would probably never admit it, Sandra felt the actual physical clearing of the site would be too much for him, especially on top of all his other duties. Nor did *she* feel equal to shifting earth and heavy debris, though she rather suspected that was what Dorian had in mind for them.

She had decided she could well afford to pay for the necessary work. Geoffrey had left her well provided for. There was money in trust for the twins. One thing she stipulated was that Dorian should not know she was paying for the work. She wasn't looking for gratitude, though it might be more difficult to keep her involvement hidden from the sharp-witted, keen-eyed Nonie than from her nephew. Especially if a gang of men were suddenly to appear and start shifting earth and laying concrete and turf. I shall just have to be as mystified as she is, Sandra decided.

So it was arranged that the landscape gardener should drive over to Vicar's Oak during the coming week and make a discreet appraisal of the site, and fortunately for Sandra's plans, Dorian was far too busy during the ensuing two weeks to think about the churchyard. There were few weddings in his church but there were still christenings and funerals, plus a summons to visit his diocesan bishop on the second Thursday.

'He only sends for me when he's got a bone to pick,'

Dorian groaned. 'It would be Thursday too. My only free day this week.'

Thursdays seemed to come around swiftly, and with them the Sewing Circle. Much to her own private amazement, Sandra had succeeded in persuading Amber to join the group and—after an initial surprised silence—one or two of the younger wives fell into conversation with her.

On the last two occasions, Mrs Faversham had not been to the vicarage. There had been no more invitations for Sandra to visit her at the Manor and she was beginning to think the original invitation had been prompted by *noblesse oblige.* But she found she had misjudged the older woman.

'My dear Sandra,' Molly Faversham said as soon as they were settled with their needles. 'You must think me awfully rude. I had fully intended to telephone you and ask you to come up and see me again. Perhaps to come at a weekend and bring your lovely children with you. But we've had guests. The Carstairses are old family friends so I do enjoy having them. But nearly two weeks of them was rather wearing. Dear Deborah is so energetic.' Certainly Molly Faversham looked pale and exhuasted, Sandra thought.

'Then you certainly won't be wanting any more visitors for a while,' she said, 'especially not two children.'

'Oh, but I understand your two are so nicely behaved. Do please come up with them tomorrow afternoon, after school. The house needs to hear children's voices and footsteps again.' She sighed. 'They grow up too fast.'

Once more Sandra found it impossible to refuse. She didn't want to refuse, but she didn't want Griff to think she had accepted in the hope of seeing him again.

But the next day the children did not go to school. Nor did they accompany her to the Manor. Leo had developed a nasty summer cold and while he was not really ill, he tended to be cranky. Certainly if he was not well enough for school he was in no fit state to go visiting, and Anna refused point-blank to go anywhere without him. Not even the inducement of farm animals could move her.

'Uncle Griff said twins should always stick together.'

Just lately Sandra had been getting a bit fed up with having 'Uncle Griff' quoted at her. His name seemed to be often on the twins' lips, as they demanded when he was coming to see them again. If she were to admit the truth, she thought wryly, her irritation was prompted by her own chagrin that he hadn't been near the vicarage since their last encounter. Craftily she suggested to her daughter, 'If you come with me you might see Uncle Griff.'

But not even this incentive could shift Anna from her determination and that afternoon Sandra set out alone once more.

Mrs Faversham was disappointed not to see the twins.

'Griff was going to show them around the Home Farm. He thought they might enjoy seeing the young animals.'

To Sandra's dismay Griff, immaculately suited, had been there at his mother's side to greet her, and though he had been called away to the telephone almost immediately, she understood he intended to spend the afternoon with them. When he returned, his face wore a wry expression.

'Mrs Carstairs! She thinks she may have left her

charm bracelet here. Though how the devil she could overlook a thing like that, I can't imagine. I've sent Meredith up to check, but she wants a word with you while she's waiting.'

'Oh dear.' Mrs Faversham looked vexed, then she brightened. 'I know, dear, while I'm talking to Deborah, Griff can show *you* around. Perhaps you won't want to see the animals, but you might be interested in his little project.'

Left alone with Griff, Sandra looked warily at him.

'Please don't feel obliged to entertain me,' she told him a little defensively.

'What?' he exclaimed with mock horror. 'When I've put this afternoon aside at my mother's special request? She seems very anxious that we should improve our acquaintance, and I'm a very dutiful son.' He made a gesture towards the open french windows. 'Shall we?'

'Where are we going?' she asked as he ushered her into the passenger seat of the Land Rover. She still felt uneasy that he should have been forced by politeness into escorting her.

'Where else but to look at my project, as Mamma insists on calling it.' Wryly, 'I don't think she takes it very seriously.'

'But you do?' Sandra recognised the road. It led to the scene of her first encounter with Griff Faversham. Soon afterwards they turned off the road along what seemed to be a surprisingly well made up farm track, and she saw that they were approaching the hop fields she had glimpsed on her journey down.

'This is part of your estate?' she asked in some surprise.

'Yes. A lot more of it used to be devoted to the growing of hops in my grandfather's day. But there's not so much call for them these days, not like there was in his time.'

'They're used in brewing beer, aren't they?' Sandra asked as the Land Rover halted and Griff jumped out. She was thankful she knew that much at least and could show an intelligent interest. So often with Geoffrey and his friends she had been made to feel unintelligent. She never felt that sense of inferiority with Griff, she realised.

'Yes.' He came round to the passenger side of the Land Rover and proffered a hand to help her down. 'But now there are chemical substitutes for the flavouring and preserving qualities traditionally provided by the hops. So there's been a steady decline in the quantities needed by brewers. And there's not much outlet in the way of export these days. Foreigners don't want English hops any more. Their beer-drinking tastes have developed along different lines.'

Sandra allowed him to take her hand and then to usher her across the rough ground. His touch seemed purely impersonal but she was, nevertheless, very aware of the warmth of strong fingers clasped about her arm, quickening her heartbeat despite her efforts at composure.

'Doesn't that mean this is a rather uneconomic enterprise?' She would have expected a man of his standing to be concerned with efficiency and monetary return. She was glad when he released her, the uneven terrain safely behind them. His touch had the power to make her oddly nervous.

'No, the small amount we grow here has an outlet, among a few local brewers who prefer to stick to the traditional methods. If that wasn't so I'd have to consider turning the land over to an alternative use.

Even as it is my friends and family think it rather quixotic of me to maintain the hop fields at all.' They were walking now alongside the rows of young green bines. 'But hop-growing has been in our family since the seventeenth century.'

Hard-headed and practical himself, Geoffrey would have called Griff Faversham a sentimentalist. But Sandra rather liked that in him. It was possible for men to be too lacking in sentiment.

'And do you use the traditional methods?' she asked.

'No,' with a wry smile, 'that might be considered riding my hobbyhorse too far. Fifty or sixty years ago, these fields would have been full of people. Nowadays it only takes one or two tractors and a few dozen people to cut the bines and feed them into machines. Sadly, it's put an end to a chapter of Kentish history quite unlike that of any other county.'

'And you regret that?' Sandra looked up curiously at the rugged face then wished she hadn't as the green eyes met hers and she felt the magnetic pull this man seemed able to exert without any effort of will.

'No. I accept progress. But then this isn't entirely a commercial enterprise with me. Hop-growing has a fascinating history. I could tell you a lot more. But you'd be bored.'

'I wouldn't,' she protested. She had a thirst for knowledge.

'Most people are bored.'

'But I'm not most people.'

'No, you're not, are you?' he said thoughtfully and succeeded in provoking a blush.

'I mean,' she said hastily, 'that I would be interested in hearing more about hopping. Since leaving school I feel that my education has been almost at a standstill.'

'Oh?' The eyebrows were quizzical and she felt bound to enlarge on her statement. She didn't want him to think her an utter moron.

'It was because of the type of people my husband mixed with,' she explained earnestly. 'The men talked business all the time, or politics. But with the women it was the latest fashions or the latest rumour in their social world. We never talked about anything *interesting*. I would have liked to go to evening classes, but Geoffrey didn't want that.' She bit her lip. She had never liked women who complained about their husbands and Griff would probably think badly of her now for sounding bitchy.

But his smiling acknowledgement of her statement gave no indication of his thoughts. He steered her in the direction of the conical-roofed oasthouses, their white cowls pointing in the direction of the wind.

'All right. We'll start with the drying houses. The drying of hops was quite a specialist job in the old days, but it was no sinecure. The dryer had to be on duty nearly twenty-four hours a day, sometimes for a whole week at a time, to make sure the fires were kept at an even temperature and that the hops dried evenly to just the right texture. The houses didn't appear as we know them until late in the eighteenth century. This one,' he indicated, 'I've converted into a small museum. It's open to the public, if anyone is interested enough to visit. And quite a few do come.'

The circular walls enclosed showcases which held old photographs and other memorabilia of former hopping days. On the wall were implements which would have been used in earlier centuries. Griff pointed to a series of the photos.

'Hopping was a colourful occasion in my grandfather's time. The fields would have been full of people—most of them Londoners. Though some would have been itinerant gypsies.' And as Sandra studied the faces, some smiling, some suspicious of the camera, 'Many London families came to the same farms year after year, generation after generation. In some instances long-standing friendships were formed with the farmer and his family. But in a lot of cases the villagers dreaded their arrival. Local shopkeepers used to put their wares behind barricades and the publicans put away their good glasses.'

There were more photographs showing hoppers standing outside long brick buildings, the accommodation farmers had been bound by law to provide for their workers.

'In the early days conditions used to be pretty rough. But just before the first war things were beginning to look up. There was greater attention to health and hygiene.'

'These photos look more modern,' Sandra commented, moving on to another showcase, partly because she was fascinated anyway, but also because Griff was leaning a little too close to her and the warmth of his masculinity was affecting her as it had done almost from the first moment of their acquaintance. In the last month of her marriage, disgust at Geoffrey's behaviour had effectively killed all physical desire on her part. Yet here she was, she thought wonderingly, so easily disturbed by a man she scarcely knew.

'Yes. After the two world wars, the hoppers were a different breed. Some, as you can see, were quite well dressed. They came down in their own cars or lorries, instead of on the hoppers' specials—trains,' he explained. 'Besides, after the second war, the Londoners were heroes of the blitz, deserving of respect.'

Yet more displays were devoted to the ancient history of hops, including the first recorded mention.

'The Roman naturalist Pliny talks of hops,' Griff said, 'so quite probably the first hops in Britain were brought over by the Romans. They used them as a vegetable, a bit like the way we eat asparagus.'

'So they wouldn't have used them for brewing beer, then? Whose idea was that?'

'I don't know. But the deliberate cultivation of them as a farm crop was introduced to England in the fourteenth century. Edward III had Flemish weavers brought to England. They had a taste for the lighter, clearer continental beer and rather than import all their beer they taught the local farmers to grow hops so they could brew their own. And talking of brewing,' he consulted his watch, 'I imagine my mother will be waiting for us with a teapot at the ready. If you're still interested, back at the house, in the library, I have a whole lot more literature on hopping.'

'I'd like that very much. But not now perhaps. I am supposed to be here to see Mrs Faversham.' Then she flushed with embarrassment. It might have sounded as though she were angling for another invitation, or, worse, another opportunity to see him. She stole an apprehensive glance at him. The Griff she had met two weeks ago would have made some teasing comment to that effect. She was sure of it.

But there wasn't the slightest flicker of change in his face as he agreed gravely that they must indeed devote the rest of the afternoon to his mother.

A little disconcerted, Sandra accompanied him back to the Land Rover. She was frankly puzzled by his restrained manner towards her, puzzled and slightly piqued. Both Nonie and Dorian had declared Griff was not one to bear a grudge, but Sandra wasn't totally convinced that he had forgiven her unwitting gaffe.

'What are you thinking about?' The question came abruptly, as the Land Rover swung out of the hop farm and on to the country lane once more. If his words hadn't come so sharply, startling her from her reflective mood, Sandra might have had the wit to prevaricate. As it was she simply told the truth.

'About you.' And then, as with a quizzical sidelong glance he muttered, 'I'm flattered,' she said, 'I mean, I was wondering if you're still offended with me.'

'Now why should you think that?' He sounded vastly interested.

But Sandra was warier now. Already she was regretting her impulsive honesty. If she explained the reason for her doubts Griff might see it as an open invitation to resume his earlier behaviour, and she didn't want that because the way he had treated her then had been the way a man behaved towards a woman with whom he hoped to have an affair. But, she thought, she would have no objection to his respect, his friendship. She regretted the fact that, in spite of her apology, she seemed to have forfeited that. Or was she being unduly sensitive?

Unable to think of a suitable answer, she could not have foreseen the results of her silence. The Land Rover veered suddenly over towards the side of the road. Griff cut the engine then shifted sideways in his seat to look searchingly at her.

Startled by the suddenness of his action, she turned her head towards him, found herself unable to hold that penetrating glance.

He repeated his question to the perfection of her profile.

'Why should you think that?'

Sandra became very absorbed in the study of her own hands, restlessly twisting the gold band on the third finger of the left. In profile her nose was small and straight. Her downcast eyes were hidden by translucent lids whose lashes swept the curves of slightly flushed cheeks. The soft, full mouth that had a fullness hinting at dormant passion had fallen into wistful lines.

Strong lean fingers enclosed the softly rounded chin and turned her head towards him. She managed to restrain the nervous little gasp that rose to her lips, but she knew the pulse beating too quickly at the base of her slender throat must be all too visible.

'Is it because I didn't follow up my intentions to take you out?' Oh, he was shrewd, this one.

'No! Oh, no!' she denied, hoping she sounded convincing to him at least. 'I didn't want . . .' Again the fascinatingly delicate lids fluttered down, but though she might hide her eyes from him she could not hide her face. His grasp would not allow it.

'It wasn't disinclination,' he told her quietly, 'but lack of opportunity.'

'I *told* you,' desperately, 'I didn't . . .'

'My mother may have told you? We had guests, friends of long standing. Any free time I had was devoted to them. But,' softly, 'their visit is over now. Sandra?' On a note of enquiry, 'Will you come out with me one evening?'

With sudden determination she freed her chin. 'No!'

'Why not?'

'Because you're asking me for the wrong reasons.' Inwardly Sandra deplored her answer. All Geoffrey's years of training in diplomatic evasiveness had gone for nought. Perhaps because it was foreign to her nature and Geoffrey wasn't around any more to reprimand her. For once she would have been grateful for a little natural guile. But her answer seemed to afford him some amusement.

'Well, that's a new one anyway.' Deprived of her chin, his hand sought one of hers in a warm strong clasp. 'So what do you think is my reason for asking you?'

Sandra shrugged. She had begun honestly. She might as well continue truthfully.

'Because you think that's what I expect, and you're wrong. I don't expect—anything . . .' She ended somewhat incoherently, for the hand that covered hers was moving over it in an absent-minded caress. She was headily aware of a virility that charged the air about her. This man stirred every nerve she possessed.

'And if I were to say you're wrong? That I'm asking you because that's what I want?'

Now her eyes, large and grey and of a startling honesty, ventured to meet his again.

'I wouldn't know whether or not to believe you. You might just be being polite.'

'My dear girl.' His laugh was a little exasperated, but he did not remove his hand from hers. 'Life's too full and too short to spend it being "polite" to women one doesn't fancy. Do you intend to come out with me or not?'

Sandra continued to regard him doubtfully. The word 'fancy' implied all that she deplored. She didn't want to be 'fancied'. She wasn't sure in fact what she did want. Frankly she was annoyed and not a little puzzled by her own inconsistency. When she had thought he was still secretly displeased with her, she had been anxious to regain his regard. But . . .

'Do I have to decide now?' she said finally.

It was difficult to analyse the expression on his face. His features betrayed nothing. Only his eyes were steady as he looked long at her, then:

'No,' abruptly, 'you don't have to decide now.' He released her hand and restarted the vehicle. 'That tea will be getting cold.'

It was only a short drive back to the Manor, and by the time they pulled up outside the front door Sandra had still not sorted out her feelings and it took all her best efforts to listen and answer intelligently as Mrs Faversham chatted over the tea-table, as the small elderly woman asked her what she thought of Griff's 'hobby'.

'I think it's a very worth-while idea. I've always thought it was a shame old traditions should die out.'

'I've promised to show Sandra the rest of my collection,' Griff said. 'Strangely, the idea doesn't seem to appal her.' He chuckled and she looked at him uncertainly.

'Good!' Molly Faversham beamed. 'Why don't you stay for dinner as well, Sandra? Then you could look at his blessed old papers this evening.'

'Oh, no,' she demurred. 'I couldn't do that. I don't like to leave Leo too long when he's feeling poorly. And I have to help get Amber to bed. I mustn't forget why I'm here.'

'But you will come to dinner another evening?' Mrs Faversham pressed, and would not be satisfied until she had Sandra's agreement.

'By the way, Griff,' Mrs Faversham said, 'Meredith found Deborah Carstairs' bracelet. Under the bed, if you please, I shall have to speak to Susan. That bracelet would have been found days ago if she'd done her job properly. Next time you're in Godmersham will you post it to Deborah for me?'

Now she was no longer alone with Griff, Sandra felt more relaxed and she was able to enjoy the conversation. Mother and son made no secret of their great affection for each other. Though obviously still frail, Mrs Faversham was looking less tense and unhappy these days, she thought. Of course the old lady would never forget her late son, but as time went on the grief must become less intense. Only once over tea did they touch on the sombre subject, when Mrs Faversham brought up the matter of a memorial plaque she was planning for Gerald.

'The Vicar asked me to let him have my suggestions. He has to submit them to the church authorities for approval.' To Sandra, 'I'd be very grateful, dear, if you'd take the design with you when you go.' To Griff, 'Do you want to see what I've put?' She sounded a little hesitant, Sandra thought, and looking at Griff she saw a nerve jump suddenly in his cheek.

'I suppose I'd better.' He sounded reluctant.

Mrs Faversham jumped up and went to an exquisite Sheraton writing-desk in a corner of the drawing-room. She brought back an envelope from which she extracted a single sheet of paper.

'Would you like to look too?' she asked Sandra when Griff had read without making any comment. 'Please,' she went on as Sandra hesitated, 'I'd like your opinion.'

The tablet and the inscription proposed were simple. The wording read:

'To the memory of Gerald Faversham (Gerry) beloved son of Molly and the late Griffiths, and brother of Griff. Sadly missed.' There followed the dates of his birth and death. As Sandra murmured appropriately, Mrs Faversham said,

'I didn't think it was necessary to put how he died.' She was still regarding her elder son with some anxiety.

'I should damned well hope not!' Griff's manner was almost violent as he rose and put down his teacup with a clash that made the fragile china ring. 'Excuse me!' He turned on his heel and strode from the room.

'Oh, dear!' Molly Faversham's face crumpled in distress. 'Griff gets so upset at the mention of how poor Gerry died. He blames himself terribly you know.' And at Sandra's look of incredulity, 'They'd had a terrible row that evening.' Mrs Faversham rose and walked to the fireplace. She took down a framed photograph which Sandra had noticed before, but had never liked to study. 'There was a New Year's ball over at Godmersham.' Absently, Mrs Faversham caressed the ornate frame. 'Griff went of course and Gerry was there—with Amber Hartoch. Of course everyone knew something was going on between the two of them. But they'd never been quite so indiscreet before.' She brought the photograph back to the sofa and placed it on the table where Sandra could see it. Gerald Faversham had been handsome, but there was something weak about the features, very unlike Griff's. 'Griff took Gerry to task.' Mrs Faversham shook her head at the photo as if her son stood before her to be reproved. 'Gerry'd had quite a bit to drink. He stormed out, taking Amber with him. It was that very nasty spell of weather we had over Christmas and New Year. The roads were treacherous.' Mrs Faversham faltered. But there was no need for her to say more.

Sandra understood now Amber's strident claim that Griff had been responsible for ruining her life. But even more she understood his reaction to her own accusation. But he couldn't possibly be blamed for the conjunction of circumstances that had caused his brother's death. She told Mrs Faversham so.

'I know that, dear, and perhaps Griff does, in his heart of hearts. But he kept saying, after the accident, that if only he'd waited until Gerry got home to speak to him, he might not have driven so recklessly, the accident might never have happened. It haunts him.'

As Sandra took her leave in the hallway Griff emerged from a door further down the hall. Tall, remote, cold-faced. Only his eyes showed signs of emotion, and Sandra felt a wave of compassion swamp her at their haunted look. She felt she wanted to go to him and put her arms about him, just as she had done many times to Leo. She wanted to comfort him, tell him he couldn't take the blame for his brother's tragic accident. But, strangely stirred as she was by these emotions, she could only stand there, racked by the oddest sensations as he moved towards them.

'Now, Sandra,' Mrs Faversham said, 'it won't be too long before we see you here again, will it? And next time I hope the children will be with you. Griff will run you back to the vicarage, won't you dear?'

'Oh, no.' She wasn't ready to be alone with Griff again just yet. She didn't want to be pressed for a decision. To Griff she said, 'Please, you mustn't bother. It isn't far to walk.'

'Of course I'll take you.' Griff cut across her disclaimers. 'Besides, I may as well see Dorian myself, about the memorial. And there are other things I'd like to discuss with him.'

Sandra was scarcely given an opportunity to say goodbye to Mrs Faversham, as Griff took her elbow and propelled her across the forecourt to the waiting Land Rover.

'I do have another vehicle,' he told her with a sideways grin, as they swept down the drive, 'in case you're wondering if I'll always be taking you out in this. But it's so handy for country lanes.

She hadn't agreed to go out with him yet, Sandra thought. She had been doubtful since she'd known who he was, since she'd seen his home. So far as wealth and sophistication went he was in a far higher league than ever Geoffrey had been.

CHAPTER FIVE

WHILE Griff was closeted in the front parlour with Dorian. Sandra checked on the twins. Leo was still full of snuffling cold but far more cheerful. Anna was her usual contented small self. So Sandra went next to see if she could do anything for Amber.

Now the days were growing warmer, Dorian wheeled Amber out into the garden on to the small patio which caught the sun for an hour or two before dinner. He had struggled to keep this free of weeds. But even so it was not a particularly cheerful prospect for an invalid, Sandra thought, and she resolved to do something about it. No time like the present. She stooped and wrenched a few unsightly plantains from the crevices between the paving stones.

'Enjoy your afternoon with the nobs, did you?' Amber enquired provocatively as soon as Sandra was within earshot.

'Very much, thank you. Don't forget you weren't altogether averse to their company at one time.' Sandra had discovered that to reply in kind was more effective with Amber than a mild answer. And indeed the other girl laughed shortly, as Sandra looked up from her task.

'Ah, but that was Gerry! He was a sweetie—a bit of a kid, but he was fun and . . . Well, I'm sorry he was killed.' Though she glared defiantly at Sandra her mouth trembled.

'Of course you are,' Sandra agreed gently, returning

her attention to the weeds, 'That's only natural. Anyone would be. And you *were* fond of him?'

'Yes, I was—in a way.'

'Enough to risk breaking up your marriage?' Sandra probed as delicately as she now eased weeds from among some colourful creepers.

'By then there wasn't much to break up. What's the use of being married to a man you hardly ever see?' Amber demanded. 'For all the need Dorian has of a wife, he might as well have been a Catholic priest, not a vicar.'

'Oh, come on, Amber!' Sandra remonstrated with her. 'You must have realised when you married him just what his work would entail?'

'Oh, yes. And I had noble visions of myself as his invaluable little helpmeet,' Amber said bitterly. 'Carrying broth to the sick like Lady Bountiful. Talking over his parishioners with him. Him asking my advice about their problems.'

'Well, I *am* surprised!' Sandra had formed the impression that Amber had always been totally self-centred, that she resented Dorian's profession just because it did engross so much of his attention, not that she had wanted to share in it. 'So why didn't it work out that way?' she pressed, sitting back on her heels to watch the other girl.

'What? With Nonie around?' The pretty young face was mutinous. 'Nonie, the ex-vicar's wife, who knew backwards how a parish should be run. What use was *I* to him?'

'You were—are—his wife.'

'More like a mistress!' Amber was restless in her wheelchair. 'Just kept for bedtime! I had no say in the running of his home. Nonie shopped, Nonie cooked, Nonie cleaned. Everything was done her way, the way she'd always done it. And Nonie was always there, talking about Mrs This and Mr That, who'd been born, married, buried. No wonder the only time Dorian had for me was in bed.'

'I thought when you got married you didn't mind Nonie living with you?'

'I didn't mind her living here. What I didn't realise was that she'd continue to rule the roost.'

'Didn't you ever say anything to Dorian? He doesn't strike me as being unapproachable.'

'How could I?' Amber demanded. 'He thinks the sun shines out of his Aunt Nonie. And she feels the same way about him. She gave up her own home to come and live with him. What was I supposed to say? Get rid of her? Pension her off? How could I do that?' Some girls wouldn't have been deterred by such considerations. Sandra's respect for Amber increased.

'They're fond of each other, of course,' she agreed. 'But you're his wife. He loves you too.'

'He did!' Amber retorted. 'But do you think he does now?'

'I'm afraid Dorian is the only one who can tell you that.'

'Well, he doesn't—love me, I mean. He hasn't told me so, not in so many words. But he doesn't have to. I have a roof over my head, food and clothing. He carries me up and down stairs. But apart from that, he doesn't touch me. Oh, Dorian will always do his duty, especially now I'm likely to be a helpless cripple for the rest of my life. But suppose I weren't? Suppose I could get up and out of this wheelchair and walk? I bet I'd be out of this house so fast, I wouldn't touch the ground.'

'Oh, come off it, Amber. I don't believe that for a minute,' Sandra said positively.

'Don't you?' Amber was scornful.

'No. I think you're being very defeatist.'

'How do you think Dorian must feel about having a wife who's the local scarlet woman? How do you think his parishioners feel, and the bishop? It's a wonder Dorian hasn't been defrocked or whatever they call it.'

'For heaven's sake!' Sandra said, suddenly exasperated. 'If you know all this you must have known it then. Why on earth did you behave like that in the first place?'

'I didn't behave like anything,' Amber exploded. 'That's the worst of it. All I wanted was to be needed. Gerry was lonely too. He needed my company. And all right, he was fun as well. We danced, we swam, we played tennis, and now,' a dry sob shook her and Sandra regretted her impatience, 'I'll never do any of those things again—with anyone.'

'And neither will Gerald!' The two girls hadn't heard Griff enter the garden. 'Has it occurred to you that *he* can't sit here and enjoy this sunshine, the company of his family and friends?' Sandra had never heard Griff's voice sound so ragged.

'Griff,' she began in an attempt to intervene, 'don't . . .' Her voice faltered as his dark scowl seemed to encompass her too.

But it was Amber he continued to address. 'Do you ever spare a thought for him in all this, for my mother's feelings?'

'Yes! Yes, of course I do!' Amber was sobbing in earnest now. 'Oh, I know you hate the sight of me, Griff Faversham, and the feeling's mutual, but I'm not what you all think I am. I'm not!'

'Amber,' Sandra pleaded, 'don't upset yourself,' and to Griff, 'Now look what you've done!'

'Amber?' It was a worried Dorian, alerted by the sound of conflict 'What's wrong? What's going on?'

Amber was incapable of answering. By this time her sobs were almost hysterical. Sandra answered Dorian but her words were directed at Griff too.

'Amber and I were having a private conversation.' At the commencement of Griff's tirade she had leapt to her feet and now she faced him accusingly. 'Griff overheard and . . . Well, whatever we were discussing, he'd no business to be listening. If he'd been a gentleman,' she added scornfully, 'he'd have pretended not to hear.'

'I'll take Amber inside,' Dorian decided. He scooped his wife up into strong wiry arms and Sandra was left alone to face Griff. But she didn't want to cross swords with him again, she thought wearily. It had happened all too often in their short acquaintance. She made to turn away, but a hand shot out, grabbing her none too gently.

'Let me go!' Her voice was husky, uneven. She was more disappointed in him than angry, but he still had the power to disturb her senses.

'Not until we get one thing straight. I thought you said you didn't take Amber's part in this.' His eyes were flinty. He was so close to her she could see the dilated pupils. Feeling stirred within her, tingling her nerve-ends. But she wouldn't allow him to intimidate her with his nearness, the emanations of his masculinity. Her grey eyes were earnest as she told him,

'Look, Griff,' she couldn't keep the anger from her voice. 'I've told you again and again I don't take sides. I'm sorry about your brother. I really am and I feel very sorry for your mother—and for you.' She ignored the impatient gesture that discarded her sympathy for

him. 'But don't you think Amber's been punished enough for her foolishness?' And as his expression remained unmoved, 'No amount of reproach can bring your brother back. She's desperately depressed. If you don't care about her, at least think of Dorian. I thought you were his friend. He's been hurt every bit as much as you and your mother.'

'He seems to have a very good friend in you too,' Griff observed wryly. 'My mother and Nonie seem to think *you* would have made him the ideal wife. Oh,' wearily, 'I'm not inhuman, Sandra. I do feel sorry for the girl but it doesn't alter the fact that she . . .'

'If you can't forgive,' Sandra said sharply, her chin tilted at him, 'then you're not the man I thought you were.'

'I'd be fascinated to know just what opinion you *had* formed of me,' he told her. His tone gave the lie to his words, but she decided to tell him anyway.

'Practically the first words anyone said to me about you,' she cried heatedly, 'were that you were one of the best, not one to bear a grudge. Dorian said . . .'

'Dorian! Dorian!' He released her arm, but her flesh still burned with his touch and their eyes still held. 'You have a great opinion of him, don't you? Tell the truth, Sandra. It's really his side you're on, isn't it?'

'I can see *everyone's* side,' she began, but he interrupted her again.

'And now I've sunk so low in your estimation I suppose you won't want to take up my invitation?'

She *was* bitterly disappointed in Griff Faversham. His own pain ought to make him more sensitive to the hurt of others. She took a tentative backward step or two.

'I'll still visit your mother. But no, I don't think it would be a good idea for me to go out with you. There doesn't seem much point, when we hold such radically different opinions.'

'Opinions? Grudge? For God's sake, Sandra!' He ran a hand through his hair, untidying its copper thickness. 'You make it sound as if we're discussing some small peccadillo. Amber was a married woman, running around with my brother. If she hadn't been . . .'

'I know!' Sandra broke in. 'If she hadn't been, you wouldn't have had a row with him the night he was killed and . . .' She stopped, appalled at what she had thoughtlessly said. 'Oh Griff, I—I'm sorry,' she faltered, as his face went rigid. 'I *am* sorry,' she repeated. 'That wasn't fair. I shouldn't have said that. I didn't think . . . I didn't mean it to sound as if I . . .' And, nervously, as Griff seemed about to take a step towards her, 'I'd better see if Dorian needs any help with Amber.' Cravenly she fled. But she took his bleak expression with her. And for the rest of the day she couldn't dismiss from her mind the fact that though she had apologised it hadn't been sufficient. She was racked by guilt and the unhappy knowledge that she wouldn't be easy until she had made her peace with him.

Dorian was standing somewhat helplessly at Amber's bedside. He seemed vastly relieved to hand his wife over to Sandra's care. From the hysterical sobbing she had lapsed into one of her sullen silences, broken only by the occasional shuddering breath.

Quietly, matter-of-fact, Sandra bathed the girl's face and administered aspirin. This time she had no need to press delicately for the other's confidence. As soon as the door closed behind her husband, Amber broke into low, impassioned speech.

'You see how it is? He can't wait to get away from

me. He'd have just the right word or action if I were one of his parishioners. But with me he doesn't know what to do, what to say.'

'Have *you* ever tried to talk to *him* about things, since . . .?'

'What can I say?' Amber asked despairingly. 'What's the use?'

'A great deal of use, I should have thought,' Sandra said bracingly as she sat down on the side of the bed. 'Telling him you're sorry might do for a start.'

'And do you think he'd believe me, any more than Griff Faversham does? You heard him. He thinks I'm just sorry for myself.'

'It's what *Dorian* thinks that matters,' Sandra emphasised. 'At least,' a little doubtfully, for she wasn't altogether sure, 'I suppose he does matter to you?'

'Yes, he does,' Amber said in a small subdued voice. 'Very much.' The hazel eyes gazing into Sandra's swam with tears, and impulsively Sandra reached out and held the other girl's hand. 'I *do* love him, Sandra. I always have. But I'm a little bit scared of him too. He's so good! I can't imagine Dorian ever being in the wrong. He should have married someone older, more sensible, someone who didn't mind sharing him with all and sundry. He must have realised that too. That's why he and Nonie treated me like a useless idiot.'

From her own experience with Geoffrey, Sandra guessed that it had been Amber's own lack of self-confidence which had given her that idea, her inexperience which had given rise to the situation. Dorian and Nonie were both far too kind to have deliberately excluded her. But it wouldn't be tactful just now to make that point. Amber needed help, not criticism.

'I think,' she said gently, 'that you've got to try and talk to Dorian. It's the only way. How can he know how you feel unless you tell him?'

'I can't. I told you. I'm scared.' She looked at Sandra with widened eyes and Sandra had no doubt that her fear was a very real one. 'Suppose I were to tell him I'm sorry, that I love him? He might say he doesn't love *me*, that I disgust him now, that he doesn't want me around any more. Then what would I do?'

'I'm sure he wouldn't do that.' Sandra tried to reassure the frightened child, for that was all Amber seemed.

'He might not put it into words. He's too kind. He might not actually tell me to get out. That wouldn't be the Christian thing to do.' There was no sarcasm or bitterness in Amber's voice. Instead there was a painful sincerity. 'But he wouldn't be able to hide his feelings from me. I think,' a little gasping breath, 'I know them already.'

'You can't know,' Sandra protested, but Amber went on almost without pause.

'Sandra.' Her eyes were huge in her pale face. 'I have to tell someone. We never did anything, Gerry and I. We were just good pals. He was lonely, I think. He was shy, uncertain of himself. He'd had a row with his girlfriend. He wasn't what Griff and his mother wanted him to be. I could understand that, because I could never please my father and I felt I'd failed Dorian too. I know people thought, and I suppose I was a fool, I let them think . . . I wanted Dorian to be jealous. But it didn't work out that way. If he even noticed he didn't seem to care or understand.'

Sandra tightened her grasp on the other girl's hand.

In her earnestness her own eyes filled with sympathetic tears.

'Amber, *I* understand. I really do. I thought I'd failed my husband too. But I was wrong. I know that now. It takes two people to make a success of marriage. Once Dorian knows you didn't do anything really wrong, that you do love him, I'm sure everything will be all right. But you *have* to tell Dorian what you've told me. You have to make him understand.'

'I can't,' Amber whispered. 'I can't. Oh, Sandra, will you talk to him—tell him?'

Aghast, Sandra stared at her.

'Oh no! It would be too embarrassing, I hardly know Dorian. Besides, I wouldn't want him to know you'd been discussing your marriage with me. This is something you have to do for yourself, Amber.'

'Sandra, please!' It was a despairing cry. 'Oh, I wish I'd had someone like you to talk to before. Maybe none of this would ever have happened.'

Looking at the strong lines of the wilful little face, albeit crumpled now into woe, Sandra doubted that the other girl would have listened to her advice. She had been younger than Amber when she had married Geoffrey and she hadn't listened to her friends or her parents. It was more likely that Amber had been due for a rebellion of some kind. Repressed by a stern father, seeing marriage and Dorian's love as a way out of her problems, the reality had not come up to her expectations. However unwitting her offence, Nonie's regime must have seemed no less rigid than that of Amber's father, herself once more reduced to a cipher.

'Sandra, please, please talk to Dorian for me,' Amber whispered, tears once more streaming down her face, quiet despairing tears more effective than hysterics.

Sandra sighed worriedly. In all humanity she couldn't refuse to help. She was discovering, despite Geoffrey's attempt to eliminate them, she had inherited some of her mother's traits. She seemed unable to avoid becoming involved in the affairs of others. She cared too much, couldn't bear to see people unhappy. There was Amber, Dorian, and just the remembrance of Griff's taut features tore at her heart.

'All right,' she said slowly, 'I'll try,' she said. 'But he may tell me to mind my own business.'

'He won't,' Amber said confidently. 'He's too polite. And he likes you. I know he does. He should have married someone like you. Perhaps it would have been better if I'd been killed like Gerry,' Amber said, her voice tremulous. 'Then Dorian could have married again.'

'You mustn't think that way, Amber.' Sandra gave her a little admonitory shake. She was upset that the idea should even have crossed the younger girl's mind. 'Life is too precious and you're still so young. While you're alive there's always hope. You've got to believe that you can put things right with Dorian, that some day you'll walk again. Do you hear me?' she insisted. 'You must try and hope!'

The younger girl was about to make some reply, but just then Nonie called up the stairs to say Amber's dinner was ready if Sandra wouldn't mind fetching the tray.

'Dorian's out,' Nonie said, when Sandra went downstairs again, nervous about her mission. 'He made a phone call.' Indignantly, 'He shut his study door so I couldn't hear who he was speaking to. Then he just said he was going out and didn't know when he'd be back.' Nonie was hurt, Sandra thought.

Possibly it was the first time her nephew had ever failed to confide in her. Even so anxiety overrode her personal hurt. 'Oh, Sandra, he looked so strained when he came downstairs. He can't go on like this much longer. What happened just now?'

Sandra related the details of the scene with Griff, but not her subsequent conversation with Amber. That would need careful thought. The execution of Amber's commission would need exquisite tact. She was rather relieved that an immediate confrontation with Dorian was impossible; and he had not returned by the time his household retired and they were not to meet at breakfast next day either.

'I don't know what time he got in last night—or rather this morning,' Nonie said worriedly. Her eyes behind their steel-rimmed spectacles looked as though she hadn't slept much. 'And now he's gone off again. But at least I know where he is this time. He's gone up to the Manor.'

'To see Griff?' Sandra felt a pang of unease at the thought of the two men, each in his own way hurting inwardly, confronting each other. But she wasn't sure for which man she felt the greater anxiety.

'No, to see Molly Faversham, about the wording for Gerald's memorial and to arrange for its installation above the family pew. Then after that he's got one or two parish visits.'

Dorian did not appear again on Saturday; and the next day of course was concerned with services.

Dressed in her Sunday best, a matching silk blouse and skirt in a blazing shade of coral, Sandra attended morning service. She was already established in the vicarage pew when Mrs Faversham and Griff entered theirs. This was the first time they had attended a service since she had been in Vicar's Oak.

At the sight of Griff Sandra's heart leapt frighteningly and heat washed through her body. Throughout the service she was very much aware of him, just across the narrow aisle from her. She hadn't been able to put him out of her mind and she longed to know if he had forgiven her unfortunate outburst, but every time she glanced his way he seemed to be staring steadfastly ahead of him. There was no way she could get up the nerve to approach him in front of a crowd of people and afterwards she would have slipped away through the private gate into the back garden, except that Mrs Faversham, moving with surprising swiftness for her age and infirmity, intercepted her, bent on meeting Anna and Leo.

Sandra was disturbingly aware of Griff at his mother's elbow, a silent witness to their conversation. She could feel her body vibrating to the uneven beat of her heart and she was unable to give Molly Faversham her full concentration. So that when she suddenly realised Molly was inviting the vicarage party to lunch at the Manor she was at once an inner mass of nerves and contradictions. She wanted to go, wanted an opportunity to set things straight with Griff, yet she was oddly afraid of the confrontation.

'Oh, but,' she stammered to Mrs Faversham, 'won't it be too much for you? All of us . . .'

'Of course not,' the small elderly woman disclaimed. 'It won't cause me any effort at all. We have a cold lunch on Sundays and Cook always leaves enough for a regiment.'

Dorian said that of course Sandra and Nonie must accept Molly Faversham's invitation. But that he must decline since Amber could not be left alone.

The twins were delighted but Sandra felt distinctly uncomfortable, and she found she dared not look at

Griff to assess his reactions.

Over lunch Molly Faversham sprung some surprising news on them.

'My doctor, ably abetted by my son,' she looked fondly at Griff who grinned back, 'has persuaded me to go on a cruise. They think it might do me good. Nonie, will you come with me, as my companion? I'd be far too nervous to go alone. So please don't be offended if I offer to pay your expenses.'

At first Nonie demurred. She couldn't possibly leave Dorian and Amber. But here Sandra intervened.

'It would do *you* good too, Nonie. And I'm quite capable of looking after things while you're away. Do go. I'm sure Dorian would say the same.'

'Dorian already knows about it,' Molly Faversham confessed with a faint flush of guilt. 'He's all for it. In fact Griff has already made the bookings for the end of next week.'

It only took a few more reassurances to persuade Nonie, and from then on the conversation between the two elderly women was of clothes suitable for warmer climes and the enjoyment to come.

With Nonie and Molly Faversham dominating the conversation lunch was not such an awkward meal as Sandra had feared. With a twin on either side of her as protection she was able to devote most of her attention to them. But even so, throughout the meal some sixth sense told her whenever Griff glanced her way and she had to repress the shivers of her involuntary response to his sexuality, the simmering energy that seemed to reach out to her. So much so that she wondered no one else was aware of the tension she felt.

After lunch, for the benefit of the twins, they toured the grounds. Then, the twins having seen the promised animals, they all returned to the house. Here Nonie said regretfully that it was time she got back to the vicarage. Knowing Nonie, Sandra guessed she was already planning the tasks she must perform before she could go away with an easy mind.

'But *you* don't have to leave yet, do you dear?' Mrs Faversham asked Sandra. 'Griff and I would be so pleased if you could stay for dinner. Then Griff could show you the rest of his . . .'

'Oh, no!' This was the chance she had needed to apologise to him and yet . . . 'I couldn't. I mean,' somewhat incoherently, 'there's the twins' bedtime.' She knew that at least one person present wasn't deceived by her hasty excuse. But it was Nonie, not Griff, who demolished it, making it look too pointed for Sandra to resist further.

'Of course Sandra must stay.' And to Sandra, 'I'll put the twins to bed for you. I shall enjoy it. I shall pretend just for a little while that they're the grandchildren I never had.'

'I wish I had grandchildren!' Molly Faversham said. Her glance at Griff was a masterpiece of reproach.

After dinner, over coffee in the drawing-room, Molly Faversham reminded Griff of his promise to show Sandra the rest of his collection of historical documents. He could scarcely refuse, but,

'Will you be joining us, Mother?' Griff asked.

'Dear me, no. I've seen your old papers dozens of times. No, there's a programme I particularly want to watch and then I shall have an early night. I'm tired. Besides I've monopolised Sandra's time enough today.' And, to Sandra's embarrassment, 'It's your turn to have her now, Griff.'

'If you're tired, perhaps it would be better if I went now,' Sandra put in. Griff obviously didn't want to be alone with her, she thought uncomfortably.

'You stay, dear,' Mrs Faversham insisted. 'Griff doesn't have enough young company, living here with an old fogey like me.'

Griff was already on his feet, but Sandra felt sure it was only compliance with his mother's wishes and not through any personal eagerness for her company. He gestured to Sandra that she should accompany him into the adjoining library. She could have refused to stay. But, she excused her weak submission, she really ought to reinforce the inadequate apology she had tried to make the other day. Besides it was also a chance to set the record straight about Amber's friendship with Gerry Faversham.

It was Dorian's right to know the truth. But for the sake of their memories of the dead man, Gerald's mother and his brother had a right to be told too. In view of the other woman's poor health Sandra had hesitated to raise the subject with Mrs Faversham. And in any case Molly had seemed so much more cheerful lately, that she had been afraid of upsetting her again. It wasn't the most delicate subject to raise with his brother but Sandra was no coward and someone had to do it.

The library, Griff's domain, was the one ground-floor room Sandra hadn't seen. Molly Faversham had explained that when he wasn't in occupation himself he kept the door locked.

'When I think of all the valuable things there are in this house!' she had said, laughing a little. 'But to Griff the contents of that library are more important than anything else.'

Sandra looked around her curiously, as Griff ushered her in. He closed the turkey-red curtains that matched the carpet, and installed her on a large comfortable leather chesterfield. The large room was lined on three sides by books, some old and battered, some expensively bound, but all, she suspected, priceless.

But not even her slow, deliberate inspection of her surroundings could still the agitated thumping of her heart. Griff Faversham had one of two effects on her. Either she was angry with him, or she was reduced to a state of quivering nerves by his proximity.

But his opening remarks dispelled all nerves and confirmed her earlier uneasy conjectures.

'I must apologise for my mother, for her blatant attempts to push us together. I'm sorry if . . .'

'So am I!' Immediately she was on her feet. 'I knew you wouldn't want me around, not after . . .'

'Sit down, Sandra!' Firmly he pushed her back into her seat. His hands, resting for an instant on her shoulders, were almost caressing. 'I didn't mean that the way you think. I'm only too pleased to have your company, if you're willing to endure mine. Truly!' as she still seemed poised for flight. 'But I don't know if you're really interested in these old things of mine, or whether you're just too polite to tell my mother and me to go to hell.'

'I am interested,' she told him, still a little stiffly. 'If you're willing to show them to me. Though I'll quite understand if you're not.' She rushed on, before he could reply, 'But in any case, I want to talk to you, if you'll listen.'

'By all means.' Disconcerting her, he moved to sit beside her, sat sideways, one arm resting along the back of the leather seat, his green eyes all attention on her face.

Embarrassed, Sandra would have risen. She would have felt more comfortable on her feet, free to move, to turn away from him. But the hand so nonchalantly resting on the chesterfield could move swiftly and once again it detained her, though not forcefully; just the contact, the sensation was enough to immobilise her.

'Stay where you are.' Ironically, 'I don't bite. Though at our last encounter you seemed in some doubt of that.'

Sandra remembered how she had fled, almost certain he was about to strike her, so unforgivable had been her words.

'That was one of the things I wanted to talk about,' she told him shakily, unable to meet the challenge of his eyes. His hand, still resting on her shoulder, seemed to scorch the flesh beneath the thin silk of her blouse and she bent her head so that her hair fell forward, concealing her face. 'I have to apologise, for what I said about your row with Gerald. I didn't mean it to sound as if I thought . . . and I wouldn't have said it if . . .'

'If you hadn't been so spitting mad with me.' There was a smile in his voice and she dared to look at him, then found herself unable to look away, for there was a smile on his face too and it transformed him. From being almost good-looking at their first encounter, he seemed to have become something considerably more in her eyes. Or was it just that she had become accustomed to his looks? 'I could have understood the mother-tiger attitude if you'd been defending one of your cubs. But I find it strange that you should take up cudgels on Amber's behalf.'

'Why? You must know I feel sorry for her, whatever she's done.'

'Frankly, because I'd have expected you to be in Dorian's corner.' The green eyes were curiously intent.

'Yes,' Sandra said frankly, not seeing how his eyes narrowed at the admission, 'I'm that too. When I met Dorian I couldn't understand how any woman could have treated him that way. He's so good, so kind.'

'Oh, undoubtedly! Dorian has all the virtues!' Griff's voice held a trace of bitterness and his hand had fallen away and Sandra felt her racing pulses slow to normal again.

'But I know Amber better now. I *like* her. And I know she's been foolish, not wicked.' She forced herself to meet Griff's eyes, even though her cheeks burned as she said the words. 'She was never—never intimate with your brother. I think you ought to know that. I think your mother would like to know that.'

'You haven't told her?' sharply.

'No! It's not an easy thing to . . .'

'Now I wonder why you find it easier to tell me.' He sounded suddenly amused.

'It wasn't—isn't easier. But someone had to tell you and,' drily, 'I doubt whether you'd have given Amber the opportunity, even if she'd had the courage to tackle you about it.' Then, 'But however I felt about Amber and her problems, however angry I was, I shouldn't have said what I did. And I can only repeat, I'm sorry.' She was unaware of the unconscious appeal in her grey eyes as she concluded, 'Will you forgive me?'

She found herself waiting breathlessly. Would he accept her apology? And if so, where did they go from here? Where did she want to go?

CHAPTER SIX

'READILY,' Griff said, and then with a sudden huskiness in his voice, 'I think it would be a very hard-hearted man who couldn't forgive *you*.' There was a pause, then, 'Well—now that's over, perhaps you'll be able to relax.' It was lightly, good naturedly said. Even so Sandra stole a doubtful glance at him. But his face did not belie the sincerity of his tone and his hand was on her shoulder again, the fingers applying a more intimate pressure this time.

'Yes,' she agreed on a long-drawn-out breath, then, resolutely meeting his eyes and with the directness that was part of her nature, 'I do so hate being at odds with anyone.'

'And we have been at odds rather frequently, you and I,' he agreed. Gently ironic, 'Do you think we've ironed out the last of our misunderstandings?'

'I hope so.' She said it with rather more feeling than she had intended and as his eyes warmed, taking on an expression she had not thought to see in them again, Sandra became very absorbed in studying her own hands. Consequently, she did not observe the rueful amusement that momentarily lit his face, followed the next instant by a mischievous gleam in the green eyes.

'And now,' he paused for effect, 'we can concentrate on the real business of the evening, can't we, Sandra?'

'What?' She looked up sharply, then coloured faintly as he waved a large hand towards his desk, spread with books and papers. 'Oh—oh, I see!'

'What,' ingenuously curious, 'did you think I meant?'

But Sandra had already jumped to her feet. Bending over the material assembled on his desk was a good excuse to let her hair swing forward, concealing her all-too-revealing face. For a few moments she had actually forgotten their reason for being in the library. For a few moments the atmosphere of the room had seemed sensually heavy, as though with emotion—that of a reconciliation after a lovers' quarrel. But she was confusing the past with the present. In the early days of her marriage that was how a quarrel with Geoffrey had been resolved. There had been apologies, the soft murmurings in each other's arms, followed by the intense lovemaking. But this man wasn't her husband. There was no earthly reason why the resolution of their differences should end in that way. But until she had moved away from him, it had almost seemed . . . A little breathlessly she said, 'This photograph.' She pointed almost at random, then wished she hadn't as he came to look over her shoulder, the warmth of his aura encompassing her in a heady wave of awareness so that her head swum with it. 'What are they doing?'

'The hoppers' wedding? It's one of a series I'm in the process of mounting. Sit down.' He pressed her into the leather swivel chair. His thigh resting on its padded arm brushed her arm as he leant forward, indicating each scene in turn. 'There were some fascinating customs observed in the old days. Though you might find some of them rather immoral.' As he spoke, his breath stirred the hair at Sandra's temple, fanning her cheek, and a strange sensation thickened her throat so that she swallowed convulsively. His words came faintly to her ears, as though from a long distance away. 'Men and women, often already married, chose hopping partners, just for the few weeks of the season. They were married by all sorts of impromptu ceremonies, and regarded themselves as perfectly free to return to their regular partners afterwards.'

The series of photographs which Sandra saw almost as through a mist showed various couples in the act of jumping over a hop-pole, while other pickers looked on.

'It's like the gypsy ceremony of jumping the broomstick,' she said, in the hope that speech might release her from the sensual thrall that had her in its grip.

'Mmn.' It could have been a sound of agreement or that of husky appreciation of her scented hair as it brushed his face. 'Some of them,' Griff told her, 'took more than one wife. Some landowners tried to stop these practices by segregation, others pretended not to notice as long as the hops were gathered efficiently.'

Despite her continuing bemusement, which had induced a sensuous languor of mind and body, Sandra was able to appreciate the variety and rarity of his collection.

'I'm gradually adding all this to the museum. I think I probably own the most representative history of hopping in this country. And only last week I bought one of the earliest models of a hop-picking machine.' She found his enthusiasm curiously endearing, but he stopped speaking abruptly and laughed. 'Look, you must stop me from going on like this. Besides,' he rose, 'I didn't get you in here just to talk about hop-picking.' He extended a hand and she regarded him warily. 'Oh, Sandra, don't shy away from me like that!' He put the hand under her elbow and urged her back towards the chesterfield. 'All I meant was that we haven't had much time for personalities, have we?' What did he mean by that, she wondered quiveringly. 'All I know about you,' he continued, 'is the little I've managed to glean from my mother.' Seating himself beside her, he looked expectantly into her face, and when his gaze centred on her lips, awareness seemed to flow across the short distance between them.

She swallowed, stirred restlessly as she tried to speak matter-of-factly.

'That's probably about the sum total of it, then. Because there isn't much to tell. Schoolgirl into wife, into mother, into widow.' She gave a little sigh. 'If I'd known what I know now I wouldn't have married so young. I feel there's so much I haven't done.'

'Places abroad that you haven't seen?' he queried.

'No, not that. We did a lot of travelling,' she told him. 'I probably know more about Europe and the Far East than I do about my own country. No, my mistake was in not having a career and in not allowing myself to develop as a person first.' Resignedly, 'I feel I'm just what my husband made me. If I hadn't married him I might have been somewhere else right now, might have been someone totally different.'

'I think that would have been rather a shame.' His tone was lightly caressing. 'I find myself liking you very much as you are, Sandra Tyler—but most of all liking you being here.' He stretched out a hand and lifted the heavy fall of hair at the nape of her neck. Sandra stiffened and his caressing movements stilled. 'We did get off on the wrong foot, didn't we, you and I, Sandra? And we seem to have been out of step ever since.' Coaxingly, 'Couldn't we begin again, hmmn?' And as she didn't, couldn't, reply, 'Sandra?' She had never imagined her name could sound like that, urgently spoken.

'Griff, please,' she begged. 'I don't want . . .'

'You don't want to be rushed.' That wasn't exactly what she meant, but he went on, 'I understand. I won't try to cut corners again. We'll take things slowly, I promise.' As he spoke, his hand had encircled the jaw furthest from him and now he turned her head towards him.

She risked an upward glance at him and saw that his attention was focused on her lips once more. She felt them quiver a nervous response and then his head came down, his mouth claiming hers, gently but masterfully. Feeling, warm and sensual, engulfed her. Many times since their first meeting she had caught herself out speculating on how it would feel to be kissed by Griff. And now her body responded as she had suspected it might—racked by a series of tremors that must be as obvious to him as to herself.

She felt a sensation she had thought forgotten, the insane longing to be held closer, to be pressed against the length of a hard male body. It was so long since she had known fulfilment, even longer ago than Geoffrey's death. For once she had known of his infidelities, she had refused to share his bed. In those days, because she had remained faithful to her vows, she had resigned herself to a life bereft of a man's lovemaking. And since she had been free she had never met a man who even remotely attracted her. She had believed the sensual side of her nature to be permanently stifled. But that was before she'd met Griff Faversham. Now she knew just how much she was missing. Not just the companionship but the physical side of marriage, the rapturous release of lovemaking.

She made no effort to evade his mouth, and she sighed rapturously as her lips opened to him and her hands crept up to caress the firm contours of his neck, then plunged into the luxuriance of the coppery hair.

'You're beautiful, Sandra. Beautiful and very desirable. God, if you only knew how just the sight of you turns me on.'

Her senses were spinning erratically. She was out of control, mindless. Only her body seemed to be functioning, sensation predominating, a throbbing need.

But despite her lack of resistance, Griff made no attempt to pull her nearer. Instead he contented himself with a series of small, teasing kisses along the softness of her throat, the line of her jaw. His teeth tantalised her earlobe and she trembled with the intensity of the feelings he was arousing. If, as he claimed, she turned him on, he must know what he was doing to her. And indeed he raised his head to look down into her flushed face, deep into the widened grey eyes, at the moist pouting fullness of her lips that longed for the further touch of his.

'Sandra,' the huskiness of his voice made her shiver, 'have you any idea what a temptation you are to me?' Then, before she could make any coherent reply, 'So much so that now I'm going to take you home, before I overstep the mark and earn your disapproval again.'

At his words disappointment stabbed painfully through her. The moments in her arms had been so brief, too brief. Surely there could be no harm in a few more kisses? Then she looked into his eyes once more, saw the banked fires that warmed and darkened their green, knew he was close to the limits of his self-control. Reluctantly, she loosened the clasp of her hands about his neck. She heard her voice, croaky, as though with long disuse, utter the trite words, 'Yes. I mustn't be too late.'

He pulled her to her feet and as he did so, his fingers crushed hers, another sign that his self-control was not as rigid as it might be. The golden wedding band dug into the softness of her flesh. She gave a little exclamation of pain and he looked down at her left hand, grimaced faintly.

'It's hard to remember sometimes that you've been married before, that you have two children. In spite of everything there's something curiously virginal about you, Sandra. Was it a happy marriage?'

'No, not really,' she admitted reluctantly, old ghosts rising to haunt her. 'My husband wanted me to be something I wasn't suited to be. He nagged me into some semblance of it. But I still failed him. Oh, yes,' she added as Griff made an incredulous sound, 'because in the end he wasn't even faithful to me.' Her tone was bitter. 'He was having an affair with his secretary. He was going away with her for one of their "weekends", when they were killed—in a car crash.'

'Did you love him very much?' The question was gently asked but with intense curiosity. Then, even more probingly, 'Were you still in love with him?'

'I was in love when we were first married. Or perhaps I just thought I was.' Sandra said it musingly, almost to herself. 'I might have gone on loving him, but when he . . . And then it was too late—I couldn't leave him, because of the twins. Even so,' she said soberly, 'it was still an awful shock when he was killed.'

'And now? You're heart-whole again? There isn't anyone else?'

She shook her head vehemently.

'No way! I'm enjoying my freedom far too much and being married to Geoffrey has taught me to be more cautious in future.' It was important somehow to make the point.

'I see.' For incalculable seconds he held her hands fast, looking down searchingly into her eyes, then, 'Let's go, shall we?'

As he ushered her out of the library, Sandra took one last fleeting look around her, as though to impress the setting on her memory. If he hadn't made the move they would have been there still. For in spite of her resolute words about caution and freedom, she knew he had awakened a hunger in her that would not be easily appeased.

The car which he had told her he possessed was long, sleek and powerful, a two-seater. Not a family car, she reflected, but a vehicle more in keeping with the image of an eligible bachelor. A confirmed bachelor? she wondered. His voice cut across her thoughts.

'Now that we've broken the ice, so to speak, can I see you again—soon?'

Her senses still fired with his lovemaking, her first impulse was to say yes. But then the sensible Sandra took over. The Sandra whose wits had not been entirely destroyed by this man's sexual appeal. She knew only too well where the attraction between them could lead and she wasn't prepared to commit herself to making love without being in love, without receiving a declaration of love. In any case Griff was wealthier, far more sophisticated even than Geoffrey had been. If and when she fell in love again she knew exactly the sort of man she wanted—an ordinary family man—and Griff didn't fit that pattern. Besides this time there was not just herself to consider. There were the twins. They needed the right kind of father. So far as Griff was concerned, she would be wise not to let their relationship go beyond light-hearted friendship.

She realised suddenly that the car was slowing and looked up expecting to see the lights of the vicarage, but the road ahead of them was dark.

'I'm not taking you home until you say yes,' Griff warned.

'Big deal!' In keeping with her recent thoughts, she tried to laugh off his sudden intensity. 'I've walked it often enough.' But tension coiled tightly within her, intensified at his next words.

'Not from here you haven't. I changed my mind, Sandra. This isn't the way home.'

'What?' She leant forward, peering through the windscreen, trying to make something out of the darkness outside.

'I found I didn't want to part with you—not just yet. And now I know my instincts were right.' He slid an arm behind her, but, panic-stricken, she resisted his attempt to draw her towards him.

With a little sound of impatience, he reached up with his free hand and flicked on the interior light, so that he could study her face. He found her wide-eyed, slightly fearful but mutinous.

'What is it now, Sandra? Is it something I've said, or done again?'

'No, it's just . . .' She took a deep breath. He deserved honesty of her. 'It's just I don't think this is a very good idea—us—you and me . . .' Her voice trailed away uncertainly as he cupped her face in strong, warm hands and she saw the attractively lazy smile that widened his mouth.

'Oh but *I* do, Sandra, I do!' Sensually his thumbs caressed her jawline.

'Griff! No! Please! You must listen. I'd like you to understand why I . . .'

'Sandra! No!' He mocked her. 'I'm not going to listen. And I do understand. I understand this!'

As his mouth captured hers, Sandra knew that for the moment at least her cause was lost. Her heartbeats accelerated, somersaulted. Her lips parted beneath his. And this time his kiss was not gentle, careful, as it had been in the library, but a feverish sensuous plundering. Their breath mingled and deep inside her a warm tide rose, causing the blood to pound in her veins. As he shifted impatiently in his seat to bring him closer to her, her hands stole up over his broad chest, finding their way inside the jacket of his suit, her fingers sliding over smooth silk that could not disguise the warm body beneath. Under her hands his heartbeat was unsteady and she felt her own trembling echoed in his body.

'You're certainly not frigid,' he murmured against her ear, the warmth of his breath as intimate as a caress. 'That wasn't what was wrong with your marriage, was it, Sandra? That wasn't how you failed him?'

'No!' It was just a stifled breathy sound as her mouth blindly sought his again.

His fingers traced the length of her backbone, moved around to slip under her blouse, stroking the soft skin of her midriff. His lips trailed from her mouth to the strained arch of her throat and Sandra moaned softly, seeking to slide her fingers beneath the fine material of his shirt. For the moment she had forgotten all her reservations about him. All she wanted was for him to touch her, love her. Her breasts had hardened, throbbed their arousal, and now his hands were discovering that fact and as she moved against him in unconsciously alluring surrender, she heard the exclamation of frustration deep in his throat.

'God, Sandra, this is impossible!' His voice was husky with desire against her throat. 'A car's no place to make love. Let's go back to the house, hmm?'

At his words, warning bells clanged loudly in Sandra's brain. For a few mad moments she had completely lost her head, forgotten everything but the throbbing needs of her body. Only now did she realise the extent of Griff's arousal, knew that if she went along with his desires and her own she would be going against all she believed in. She hadn't allowed Geoffrey to make love to her before they were married. But it wasn't just that. If she gave in to her physical feelings, gave in to him, once again she would be handing herself over body and soul to the wrong kind of man. For herself she knew physical involvement would mean emotional commitment. And she needed a marriage in which she could give as well as receive. Not one where she would be expected to conform to her husband's expectations. She stiffened, her hands pushing him away.

'Sandra?'

'No, Griff—*no!*' She said it positively this time. 'Please take me home.'

His eyes, still burningly aroused, held hers, but she met them determinedly.

'Please, Griff! I mean it.'

For an instant his hold on her tightened painfully, then he put her away from him, his voice hoarse with frustration.

'All right! Point taken! I'm going too fast for you again.' His hands gripped the steering-wheel, their knuckles white, and she sensed his immense effort at self-control. Then, tautly, '*Am* I going to see you again?'

'Griff!' Impulsively she set a hand on his arm, then

as quickly removed it as she saw the nerve that jerked in his jaw. Her words came haltingly. 'Griff, I don't think that would be wise.'

'Wise?' he snapped.

'Well, at least give me time to think,' she temporised. 'I can't think when you . . .'

'To think?' Harshly, 'About what, for God's sake? You've just shown me that you don't exactly find me repulsive.'

'Please, Griff!' she pleaded with him. 'Just give me time!'

'All right.' It came out on a long exasperated exhalation. 'All right!'

The engine sprang to life beneath impatient fingers and the long, sleek car purred away the miles back to the vicarage, without another word spoken between its occupants. But as Sandra slid from the passenger seat, Griff said warningly, 'I'll phone you tomorrow!'

The vicarage was in darkness. Guiltily Sandra realised just how late it was. Removing her shoes she stole upstairs only to be accosted at the head of the staircase by Nonie in nightdress and dressing-gown.

'Sandra! I was beginning to worry. I know it's not far to drive from the Manor, but since Amber's accident . . .' Nonie followed her into the bedroom. She sat on the edge of the bed and Sandra suppressed a sigh. Nonie, despite the lateness of the hour, was obviously disposed to chat. She was full of the coming cruise, half anticipatory, half guilty. 'And now, dear—tell me all about your evening. How did you get on with Griff?'

'Oh, all right.' Sandra was deliberately casual. 'He showed me some more of his collection of hopping memorabilia. We played some music.'

'I've been thinking, dear, wouldn't it be nice if you

were to marry Griff,' Nonie sighed sentimentally. 'I believe he's getting rather fond of you and . . .'

'Rubbish!' But Sandra forced a smile to soften the exclamation. 'A man like that who's escaped matrimony this far isn't going to pay serious attention to a widow with two children. He made his feelings on the subject of children quite clear, early on in our acquaintance. No, he's just flirting.' She stopped short of shocking Nonie's susceptibilities by telling her Griff probably only wanted an affair.

'But what about you?' Nonie asked. 'How do you feel about him?'

'I've only known him a month,' she prevaricated.

'So?' Nonie said placidly. 'I knew the first time I met my husband that he was the one for me.'

'Then you were lucky,' Sandra said feelingly. 'I don't believe in love at first sight any more. And I've been married once, remember? It's not an experience I want to repeat in a hurry. I don't want to get heavily involved with another man.'

'Not yet perhaps,' Nonie agreed, 'but . . .'

'It's not just a question of when, Aunt Nonie,' Sandra insisted, 'but who.' The doubts she had experienced in Griff's car were crystallising. 'Don't you see? Griff Faversham is the last man I ought to get involved with. He's rich—richer than Geoffrey would ever have been. You know the style they live in. I know Mrs Faversham doesn't entertain much, but she's getting on, she's not very well and she's just had a bereavement. But if Griff ever married, he'd surely expect his wife to act as hostess to his county friends. I don't want that kind of hassle again. I had enough of that with Geoffrey's acquaintances. And,' she sighed deeply, 'I wouldn't want to fail Griff as I failed Geoffrey.' If Nonie saw any significance in that last sentence she refrained from comment. 'In fact I don't think I want to see him again,' and as the older woman parted her lips as if to argue, 'Nonie,' she said apologetically, stifling a yawn, 'I'm sorry, but I'm awfully tired.' Nonie, she knew, was quite capable of chatting on into the small hours.

'Of course, dear. How thoughtless of me.'

But even with Nonie's departure, Sandra could not settle to sleep. Over and over her brain replayed the evening's conversations with Griff, while her body relived the scenes on the couch, in his car. The first kiss she might have forgotten—*might*, she mocked herself. But the second, that had lasted much longer. She put a wondering hand over her mouth, the mouth that had come so vibrantly awake to his. Mouth, the traitor, that could respond without consultation with her will. Just remembering his lips on hers sent her senses spinning out of control, her body dominating her mind. If only he hadn't kissed her. Despite what she had told Nonie, was even now trying to tell herself, she had a terrifying conviction that henceforth there would be a kind of gnawing hunger within her, for the touch of those sensual lips, the feel of those strong, masculine arms about her.

Griff was not quite like any other man she had ever met, she mused dreamily. But weren't his values just like any other man's? She could almost wish she were more experienced. But she had only had Geoffrey's example on which to base this assumption. When she was away from Griff she thought she knew what was right for her. But he had only to look at her with those wide green eyes of his, touch her, kiss her, and she seemed to lose all rationality.

But she *must* stay in control. She must draw back from danger before it was too late, before, moth-like, she was irrevocably attracted to the scorching flame of his masculinity. She had been prepared, for the immediate future at least, to dedicate herself to the twins, to some as yet uncharted course of self-improvement. Remarriage, if the opportunity presented itself, was lower down on this agenda. But meeting Griff Faversham had come perilously near to shattering these plans, close to altering her priorities.

It was a long time before Sandra fell into a heavy, unrefreshing sleep and she was tired when next morning she drove the twins to school, then set about helping Nonie with domestic chores until it was time to rouse Amber. She was determined not to dwell any longer on the events of the previous evening. Her mind, she told herself, was made up once and for all. She had only become entangled with Griff Faversham again through her bounden duty to apologise to him. Her conscience was clear on that score now, there was no need to seek him out any more.

Nonie had just suggested they pause for a coffee-break when the telephone rang and the older woman went to answer it. Sandra tensed. Her ears were strained to hear Nonie's end of the conversation. There was no reason why this particular call should be Griff, telephoning *her*, yet instinct told her it was.

'For you, Sandra dear!' Nonie returned to the kitchen. 'Griff.'

'Will you tell him I'm out, please.' Sandra went on steadily with some ironing she had appropriated from Nonie.

'Oh no, dear,' shocked, 'I couldn't tell a fib like that. Besides, I've already said you're in.'

With a sick apprehension that seemed to descend right into the pit of her stomach, Sandra went to the telephone. How ridiculous to be nervous of telling a man you didn't want to see him again. Or was she nervous rather because she wasn't altogether sure she was doing the right thing? 'Griff? Sandra!'

He went straight to the point.

'You know why I'm calling?' His disembodied voice sounded remote, stern.

'The answer's no, Griff.' She forced herself to speak calmly, matter-of-factly, glad that he couldn't see the tell-tale flush of her cheeks, the agitated rise and fall of her breasts that just the sound of his voice had induced.

'Why not, for God's sake?' His voice exploded in her ear and the anger in it made her quiver.

'I don't want to go into details,' she told him, her agitation making her voice high and strained. 'Please, Griff, just accept my decision.'

'I'm damned if I will,' he said harshly. 'I think I'm entitled to an explanation at least.'

'I just don't want to go out with you. That's all you need to know.'

'Like hell it is.' Then, seductively, 'Sandra . . .'

'No! Goodbye, Griff.' She returned the receiver to its rest before she could weaken. She stood still for a long moment until her legs had stopped shaking and she felt she could control her voice.

From the stove where she was making coffee, Nonie looked at her expectantly.

'I've told him I don't want to see him again,' Sandra said with would-be nonchalance. She could sense the older woman's intense curiosity, but she volunteered nothing further.

'I see.' Nonie sounded disappointed, then, 'The coffee's ready. Would you take Dorian's through? He's hardly got one Sunday's sermon over before he's starting on the next.'

As she traversed the long passageway to Dorian's study Sandra felt apprehensive once more, but this time for a different reason. This was the opportunity she needed to persuade Dorian of the truth about Amber, about his wife's feelings towards him, and she mustn't shirk it.

If Dorian was writing next week's sermon it wasn't progressing very well. The sheets of paper before him were blank and so was the face he turned towards Sandra. No, not blank, just despairingly empty. But in an instant a bland welcoming mask replaced the unhappiness she had glimpsed.

'Sandra, this is good of you.' Troubled he might be, but Dorian would never neglect his manners or his duty.

Sandra sat down in the visitor's chair, facing him across his desk. She came straight to the point.

'I have to talk to you Dorian. I'm afraid it's rather personal.'

'Of course, Sandra.' Whatever effort it might have cost him he was all attention. 'Advice is part of a clergyman's province. How can I help you?'

Sandra shook her head.

'It's the other way round,' she told him. Then, a little more hesitantly, 'I don't want to sound nosy or presumptuous, but I think *I* may be able to help *you*—and Amber of course.'

'My dear, you've already helped us tremendously. What more could you possibly do, unless you possess a magic wand?' Dorian pushed back his chair and walked to the window that overlooked the back garden. 'Since you came this house has had a happier atmosphere than it's held in a long time and I'm very grateful to you, Sandra.' But he went on before she could plunge into her prepared speech. 'Unfortunately we may have to leave it.'

'Oh, Dorian! Why?' She bit her lip. 'Oh, I'm sorry! That's an impertinent question.'

'My dear, impertinence is the last thing I should accuse you of. Do you remember the Bishop sending for me recently?' And as she nodded, 'Foolish of me to hope rumours hadn't reached his ears.' He thrust his hands through already dishevelled hair.

She turned in her chair to look at him, as he stood, his back turned towards her.

'You mean rumours about Amber and Gerry Faversham?' she realised. 'That's why you might have to leave Vicar's Oak?' Incredulously, 'You mean the Bishop . . .? Oh, surely not?'

'No,' wearily, 'he hasn't told me I *have* to leave. He just put it to me that I might find my present situation untenable in the circumstances.'

'You're not planning to divorce Amber or anything?' In her alarm Sandra jumped up and went to him, put a hand on his arm, scanned the tired face almost on a level with hers.

'Divorce!' Dorian was shocked. 'Certainly not. It would be against everything I believe in. On the other hand, of course, Amber may want her freedom. She seems to have been unhappy living with a dull, prosaic clergyman.' Ruefully, 'I'm no Gerry Faversham.'

'Dorian.' Again Sandra was hesitant. She was treading on very private ground, but unless she asked . . . 'Forgive me, but do you . . . are you still in love with Amber?' The look he gave her was answer enough. 'In that case, Dorian, you must talk to her now, right away. Please believe me. I think if you do everything will be all right.' And as he looked enquiringly at her. 'No, Dorian, the rest is for Amber to tell you.'

Dorian took her at her word and she heard him taking the stairs two at a time. Sandra hoped fervently that this would mean a reconciliation between husband and wife, that somehow, even with Amber's disability, the couple could rediscover their first happiness.

No one ever knew exactly what had taken place, or been said, that morning between Dorian and his wife, but the results were obvious to see. Some of the lines of strain had eased from Dorian's face, and when Sandra took in his afternoon cup of tea he took the opportunity to thank her. He stood up, rounded the desk and placed a hand on each of her shoulders.

'Without you, Sandra, we might have gone on for months, each of us reluctant to approach the other. You've been our good angel. God bless you!' He bent his head and kissed her cheek, and impulsively out of her happiness for him and his wife Sandra hugged him.

'My God! No wonder you gave me the brush off!'

Still half embracing, Sandra and Dorian looked up to see Griff in the study doorway.

'The hypocrisy of some people!' Griff's voice was harsh, filled with scorn, his eyes with some other emotion less easy to define. 'Maybe the Vicar's wife isn't so much to blame after all, when the Vicar can . . .'

'Griff!' Shocked, Sandra moved away from Dorian, took a step towards the doorway, 'Don't jump to conclusions. It isn't what . . .'

'*You* tell *me* not to jump to conclusions! Oh, that's rich! I'm sorry to have interrupted your touching little scene. And to think I credited you with integrity, Sandra Tyler.' The door banged shut behind him with a violence that reverberated around the old house.

CHAPTER SEVEN

SANDRA'S first impulse was to run after Griff, to *make* him listen, to tell him he had misunderstood the scene in Dorian's study. And she had already reached the door when second thoughts prevailed, bringing her to a halt. She had no doubt Griff had come to the vicarage to demand some explanation of her rejection of him. His misapprehension might prove a more effective deterrent than any protest she might make. And yet contrarily, she hated the thought that he had carried away with him the ugly idea that something was going on between her and Dorian. Slowly she turned away from the door.

'What on earth was all that about?' Dorian asked with genuine bewilderment, and Sandra was relieved to find that he really hadn't caught the point of Griff's remarks.

'Nothing important,' she said hastily. 'Just a misunderstanding. Forget it?'

It was all very well to tell Dorian to forget Griff, she thought unhappily. Griff's face with its look of disappointed censure would haunt her inner vision for a long time to come.

In the days that followed Amber was shyly, tentatively happy and suddenly industrious, displaying hitherto unrevealed domestic talents.

'After all, I had to run my father's home, after Mum died,' she told Sandra when she expressed surprise at Amber's very creditable pastry-making. Then, wistfully, 'If only I could walk now. Everything would be perfect. I've told Dorian he's not to think of leaving Vicar's Oak. He's no reason to be ashamed or to run away, and neither have I,' with a defiant toss of her head, 'I'll just have to live the gossip down, and with his help I will!'

'And Nonie?' Sandra asked, as she adjusted the special table Dorian had made, so that Amber could work from her wheelchair.

'Nonie and I understand each other now.'

Dorian's aunt, it seemed, had offered her own solution. While she was away on the cruise with Molly Faversham, Dorian was going to get a local builder to turn two of the large downstairs rooms into a self-contained flat for the older woman, so that husband and wife could enjoy more privacy. Nonie blamed herself, she had told Amber, for much of what had happened.

'She thought it would be too much for me, coping with everything, running a home and parish activities. She thought she was helping. She didn't realise I saw it as being pushed into the background.'

'But will you be able to afford all the structural alterations?' Sandra asked.

'Dorian says my claim for insurance compensation will be through soon.'

'Against Gerry Faversham's estate?'

'Yes.' Amber looked and sounded a little incredulous. 'Griff Faversham told Dorian today that he'd had a word with the lawyers and got things speeded up.'

'Griff did?' Griff Faversham was a constant source of surprise to Sandra. 'That was good of him, considering . . .' She stopped short with sudden realisation. 'But that means Dorian's seen Griff today?' she asked, and as Amber nodded, 'Then surely Griff must know . . .?' Again she stopped. She had been going to say that if Griff was aware of the rapprochement between Dorian and his wife, he must also know there was nothing between herself and Dorian. But she prevented herself just in time from making the *faux pas.* Yet Griff hadn't been near the vicarage, she brooded. At the very least he might have apologised. Surely he owed her that?

'About me and Dorian? Yes, I suppose so. Because Dorian saw Mrs Faversham as well. He said *he'd* tell her that Gerry and I hadn't—that we didn't . . . Dorian's a good man, Sandra. Oh, I wish I'd never . . .' Amber was suddenly tearful.

'That's all in the past now,' Sandra told her firmly, but though she adopted a bracing manner with Amber she felt far from cheerful herself, a frame of mind which not even constant activity could dispel; and there was certainly plenty to keep her busy as the next few days saw the vicarage in a ferment, the whole household involved in getting Nonie off on her trip with Mrs Faversham.

With Nonie's departure, more and more of her chores devolved upon Sandra, the shopping in particular. But even so her mind, had a tendency to keep returning to the sore point, much as a tongue cannot resist probing a bad tooth. Why hadn't Griff had the decency to apologise to her? When she had suffered from misapprehensions about him, she had made a point of apologising, whatever the embarrassment it had caused her.

It was not only the vicarage which was in turmoil.

'What in the world are those men doing in the churchyard?' Dorian demanded, coming in from his parish rounds one morning about a week after

Nonie's departure. The two girls looked questioningly at him. 'They seem to be digging it up.'

Sandra didn't need to feign surprise. She was surprised. Why, she wondered, had Mr Crosthwaite ordered work to begin when she hadn't yet accepted his quotation? She had been awaiting Dorian's decision as to whether or not he would be staying in Vicar's Oak. She hurried out into the garden and through the private gate into the churchyard. A man with a Rotavator was turning the earth. Two others were unloading paving slabs and other materials from a lorry. Casually, she strolled through the grounds, pausing to ask one of the men what was going on.

'Prettyin' up the churchyard. Seemingly the Vicar wants a rockery and some kind of rose-bower, where couples can have their weddin' photos took.'

This was undoubtedly the design she had discussed with the landscape gardener. Oh, well! Sandra shrugged. At least the Hartochs were staying, and she could well afford the figure Crosthwaites had quoted.

Dorian was pleasantly surprised, if a little bewildered, to find his plans were being executed.

'I haven't a clue who gave the orders for it. But I bet I can guess.' Sandra felt her cheeks colouring, until he went on, 'It's just the sort of thing Griff would do. Though how he got wind of what I had in mind I can't imagine.'

But still no one had seen Griff, until one Saturday morning, when Sandra had been out shopping, leaving Leo and Anna playing happily under Amber's supervision. A strong bond of friendship seemed to have sprung up between the younger girl and the twins.

'Usual shipping order,' Sandra gasped as she set the laden basket down on the kitchen table. 'Goodness knows how we manage to get through so much food.'

'Young Leo's developing quite an appetite,' Amber said. 'Haven't you noticed?'

'Yes, I have, actually.' Sandra had been astounded on one occasion to find Leo eating the scrambled eggs that Amber had put before him, eating them with relish and without a word of complaint. Leo was beginning to look sturdier, Sandra thought. The country air had done him good. He was happier, more relaxed. He referred less often to his father, and when he did it was without the accompanying tearfulness. 'And of course Anna's always eaten well,' she said aloud, then, 'Talking of the twins,' she looked around her, 'where are they?'

Amber looked suddenly self-conscious.

'They've—er—gone out. Er . . . been taken out,' she added hastily as Sandra looked anxious.

Sandra relaxed.

'Oh, by Dorian.'

'Er, no. Actually, Griff was here a little while ago.'

'Griff was! What was he doing here?' Irrationally Sandra's heart lurched at the thought that Griff had been here and that she had missed him. The next minute she was reproaching herself for foolish inconsistency. Far better that their paths shouldn't cross. She had made her decision—to have nothing more to do with him.

'He said he'd come because he thought it was time he and I had a chat, now we've patched up our differences,' Amber told her. 'As he pointed out we're going to be living in the same village for a long time, maybe the rest of our lives, and the vicarage has always had close connections with the Manor House.' Amber sounded a little bewildered. 'You know, Sandra, he's really rather nice. I'd never realised.

We—we talked very frankly about Gerry. He said you'd told him . . . Oh, Sandra,' there was a catch in the younger girl's voice. 'I owe you so much and I do realise how very lucky I am. Suddenly everything's going right, except . . .' She gestured to her wheelchair. Then, after a sigh she braced her shoulders and went on determinedly, 'But I'm going to count my blessings, not complain. And by the way, since Griff was being so friendly, I asked him if he was responsible for the work going on in the churchyard. At first I thought he was going to deny it. But then he laughed, and said since I'd guessed he might as well admit it but that I wasn't to breathe it to anyone but Dorian. Still, I'm sure he wouldn't mind me telling you.'

Sandra stared at her. How the man did seesaw in her estimation. One minute she warmed towards him and the next . . . But this was the absolute limit. She had been perfectly genuine in her intentions to remain the anonymous donor of the churchyard improvement scheme, but here was Griff, actually letting people think . . .

Something Amber had said earlier now registered with Sandra.

'Do you mean,' with angry incredulity, 'that the twins have gone off with Griff? That he's taken them out somewhere, without waiting for my permission?'

'Shouldn't I have let them go?' Amber looked worried. 'I didn't think you'd mind. I thought you and Griff got on all right.'

'It's not your fault,' Sandra reassured her. 'You couldn't know. But Griff does. He must have known I wouldn't let them go with him.

'Why? They seem to adore him, and he's very good with them.'

'Because he's just using them. Oh, he won't do them any harm,' as Amber began to look alarmed,' I don't mean he's kidnapped them or anything. But he must have a very bad memory. He must have forgotten he once told me he couldn't be bothered with kids. Now here he is pretending he wants their company, because he thinks it'll sway *me*. It's not fair,' indignantly, 'to use them like that, when he must know they miss having a man around.'

'Don't *you* miss that.' Amber asked. 'Having a man around? I would have thought, once you'd been married . . . I only know how I felt, of course, when I thought my marriage might be over. Wouldn't you like to be married again. And if Griff's so keen . . .?'

'I don't think Griff has marriage in mind,' Sandra said drily. 'Yes, I would like to marry again someday. But not to someone like Griff. Have you seen the style they live in?'

Amber shook her head.

'No,' wryly, 'I wasn't exactly *persona grata* at the Manor. But what's that got to do with it?'

'When, if, I marry again, I want a comfortable, homely life—not just for myself, but for the twins. When Geoffrey was alive, we weren't what I call a proper family. Oh, we had everything money could buy. But there was no home atmosphere, Geoffrey and I were always travelling, the twins were brought up by a nanny most of the time. I'm reasonably capable, Amber. I know I can run a house, prepare meals as well as anyone, but I hate putting on side.'

'And you think Griff Faversham would expect that?'

'I'm sure of it.' Sandra was emphatic. 'Once when I was at the Manor, Mrs Faversham showed me some photos. Some were of Griff. One or two with girls he'd been briefly engaged to. I asked her why he'd never married either of them. She said she only knew what he'd told her—that they just wouldn't fit in with his life-style. You'd only to look at them, Amber! Beautiful, sophisticated! Any of them would have made a perfect lady of the manor. If they couldn't live up to him—and by the way they were looking at him, they'd have been willing to have a try—what chance would I have?'

'I think you underestimate yourself, Sandra. I think you'd make a marvellous lady of the manor.'

'That's just what I don't want to be,' Sandra explained. 'Oh, I love the old house, and if it wasn't so elegant it would make a marvellous rambling family home. But can you really picture the twins let loose among all those priceless antiques? And then there's me. Mrs Faversham looks right in afternoon frocks, twin-sets and pearls. I can just see her taking tea with bishops and lord lieutenants and opening fêtes and things. All I want is to be a straightforward housewife and mother.' Wistfully, 'And I'd like to have at least two more children. No,' she shook her head determinedly, ' I know what I want for me and the twins. And that's why I'm so annoyed at Griff taking them out without so much as a by your leave. I don't want them getting attached to him. It will make things hard, particularly for Leo, when we have to leave here.'

'Oh, by the way, he said to tell you,' Amber put in, 'that he'd be giving them lunch at the Manor if you'd like to join them.'

'You see what I mean?' Sandra demanded irately. 'About him using them to get to me? I will go up there,' she said fiercely, 'but only because there are a few things I want to have out with Mr Griff

Faversham. If he thinks being lord of the manor means he can ride roughshod over the common courtesies, he can think again.'

She hadn't used the car since she had arrived in Vicar's Oak, but now she was in too much of a hurry to tackle Griff to walk. At the front door to the Manor she braked hard, sending gravel spurting in all directions. And her pressure on the front door bell, applied hard and long, brought Meredith, slightly less stately than usual and consequently a little reproachful of countenance.

'Mrs Tyler?'

'Where's Mr Faversham?' She stepped briskly past the butler into the large square hall, aware as always of entering a gracious but awesome environment—the richness of ancient timbers, the glow of well tended copper and brass, the fresh arrangements of hot-house flowers in antique vessels.

'At your service!' The voice came from behind her and she swung round abruptly to see Griff framed in the doorway against the sunlight which made a burnished aureole of his coppery hair. As always he was casually but expensively tailored. Her heart, as always at the sight of him, thudding ridiculously, Sandra was immediately conscious of the fact that she had taken no thought to her own appearance before rushing up here to confront him. She was aware of the fact that both the close-fitting jeans and old T-shirt she wore around the house had seen better days. Geoffrey had always criticised her love of casual, comfortable clothes. 'Why,' he had demanded, 'with all the smart expensive things I buy for you, must you always look like a charity object?' To Sandra it seemed criminal to wear good clothes unless she were going somewhere special. But Geoffrey had deplored this habit of hers, so how much more must Griff? 'I saw your somewhat tempestuous arrival,' he commented drily. Then, a mischievous glint in his eyes, 'Do you realise it takes two gardeners a whole day to rake that gravel?'

She mistook the glint.

'I'm sorry about that!' she retorted tartly. 'Sorry, I mean, that you haven't got anything more worthwhile for them to do.' Then, 'Where are my children?' she demanded.

'Quite safe, I assure you. Bradshaw, my excellent farm manager, is introducing them to the delights of mucking out and feeding the animals.' He grinned mischievously.

Suddenly Sandra's indignation, deliberately whipped up on her way to the Manor, seemed to evaporate. As usual when Griff was near, her pulses were fluttering like startled birds, the blood in her veins a restless dizzying torrent. And when he smiled at her as he was doing now . . .

'You're a little early for lunch,' he told her, 'but perhaps I can offer you a coffee?'

'I didn't come for lunch, or for a coffee.' She was trying to avoid meeting his eyes, knowing the effect his gaze could have upon her. But some strange compulsion, some deliberate magnetism which he seemed capable of exerting, forced her finally to meet their green engulfing fascination.

'Then you're here just for the pleasure of my company? I'm flattered.' And indeed his voice was warm with pleasure.

'Don't be!' she retorted, with a feeble attempt to recapture her earlier fury. 'You know very well I wouldn't have come if you hadn't made off with my children.' Uncomfortably aware of the hovering Meredith, she said, 'Isn't there anywhere else we can talk?' Then wished she hadn't, for immediately his hand was at her elbow, steering her towards the library, the room she had entered only once before, a room whose sensual memories seemed at once to wrap her about in an atmosphere of unwanted intimacy.

His gesture invited her to take a seat, but a swift glance about her confirmed the recollection of only the leather chesterfield and the swivel chair behind the desk, both of which afforded him too many opportunities for dangerous proximity.

'Thank you, I'd rather stand. I'm only staying long enough to get one or two things straight.'

'A very good idea,' he applauded. 'And a very necessary one. Alas, we seem fated, you and I, to be at odds with each other. No sooner do I think we have things sorted out, then you find some new cause for complaint against me.' It was humorously said, as if he felt no guilt at all in the matter. And there was that smile again, inviting her response.

'And whose fault do you think that is?' she demanded, prepared to be affronted, but again he took the wind out of her sails.

'Do you know,' he said confidentially, moving a little nearer to her. 'I'm beginning to wonder that myself. I have a theory, if you'd care to hear it.' He was close now, very close, so that she imagined she could feel the warmth of his body, and there was no more room in which to retreat. She felt her blood palpitate close to her skin. There was a tenseness in the set of his chin, the line of his long sensuous mouth. The moment was frozen, held in the thrall of physical attraction.

'D-don't bother to theorise,' she told him unsteadily. 'I can tell you.'

'Oh, don't take all the fun out of it. Let me guess!'

And before she could interrupt, 'Such antagonism as you seem to feel for me can only be due to one of two causes. Either you're madly in love with me,' Sandra gasped indignantly, 'or you genuinely find yourself unable to like me. Now,' the green eyes were laughing a challenge at her, 'which shall I settle for?'

She would have liked to be able to say the latter and mean it. But Sandra recognised that it was only half the truth. There were things about him which she found herself unable to accept, but only, she realised suddenly, because of their effect upon her—things that if she were totally indifferent to him wouldn't matter. She didn't dislike him. But she wasn't, she told herself firmly, going to fall in love with him.

'Do you know,' Griff continued thoughtfully, 'I don't believe you dislike me. There seems to be too much evidence to the contrary.'

Evidence? What was he talking about? She was not left long in doubt. His arm shot out and encircled her, held her so determinedly that none of her struggles were of avail. Slowly, inexorably he lowered his mouth to hers. His lips on hers were insistent, warm, sweet, increasing the turmoil within her blood. She fought against the sensation. But his kiss deepened, the pressure of his body against hers hardening. And instead of continuing to resist she felt herself go limp against him, her lips parting, and then his hunger had communicated itself to her. His kiss was a sensuous exploration. His heart was beating violently beneath the hands she had raised to ward him off. Slowly her arms crept round his waist, her body curving submissively to his, and she was conscious of little sensual sounds emanating from her own throat, as his thighs, hard and warm, fired a response in her. When, finally, he lifted his head, for a moment neither of them said a word. Sandra's pulses clamoured wildly as his eyes held hers in a long, intense stare, his a darker green than she remembered, reflecting not only amusement, but something else, something which made her swallow and renew her attempts to free herself.

'Let me go . . .!' she begged.

'First tell me you dislike me,' he said at last. 'Convince me—as you've just convinced me of the opposite.'

She couldn't tell him that, but to admit the opposite . . . The possible results didn't bear thinking about. There had to be some way out of this Catch Twenty-two situation. She sought vainly for words.

'You don't dislike me,' he reaffirmed since she seemed incapable of speech. 'But I've obviously committed some offence.' He released her and she ought to have been relieved. Instead she felt oddly deprived. 'I think you'd better sit down after all, Sandra,' he told her. 'This is going to be a longer session than I thought. Because you're not leaving until you've given me a chance to defend myself.'

'You can't keep me here against my will,' she said a little wildly. 'And I want my children.' She made a movement towards the door but he intercepted her.

'*Sit down*, Sandra,' he commanded. 'Leo and Anna will be occupied until lunch time, which is still a good way off. As for keeping you here,' he moved towards the door, locked it and pocketed the key, 'rather theatrical, I know,' he said with a wry grin, 'but since you will insist on casting me as the villain of the piece . . .'

Sandra panicked. What had he got in mind?

'Unlock that door at once!' she demanded. 'You've no right . . .'

'None whatsoever,' he agreed urbanely. 'But what exactly do you propose to do about it? I can't see you being undignified enough to scream the place down. Of course,' he grinned wickedly, 'you could try and get this key from me. That might be rather enjoyable.'

Sandra had the sense to know when she was beaten. No way was she going to approach him and engage in physical combat. There was only one way, she realised, that such an encounter could end; and whilst inwardly she quivered, imagining, tempted by the thought of that outcome, her logical brain was still sufficiently in command to reject it.

'All right,' she said, 'I'll sit down.' Then, unwisely she realised as a look of awareness sprang into his eyes, she added, 'If you stay away from me.'

'So!' it was a pleased drawl, 'you're still afraid I might be able to influence you to the contrary? OK, Sandra, we'll play it your way. Let's say I won't lay a finger on you again or even come near you unless you yourself ask me to.' As Sandra perched herself on the edge of the chesterfield, he leant against his desk, one long leg crossed over the other, arms folded, his gaze implacable. 'Shoot!' he invited.

Confronted now with the necessity of prosecuting, Sandra felt all her former initiative drain from her. But his expression was implacable and she knew he was quite capable of carrying out his threat and keeping her here indefinitely.

'F—first,' she stammered, 'you thought Dorian and I were . . .' He wasn't going to help her at all, she realised as he remained expectantly silent. 'Then, when you must have known it wasn't so, you never called me to apologise. At least when I was mistaken about you,' her indignation rose, 'I had the grace to admit I was wrong.'

'Is that all?' He didn't sound at all penitent. 'The only reason you haven't had your apology, Sandra, is that I've been away. I went up to Norfolk, to an exhibition of farm machinery. So I've had no opportunity until today. And you haven't given me much chance yet, have you?' he pointed out, but she refused to be placated that easily.

'You could have written.'

'True,' he admitted, his eyes holding hers with devastating effect, 'but with you and me, Sandra, it's always been so much fun making up face to face. In fact,' suggestively, 'I'd been rather looking forward to it.'

So had she, Sandra realised with a sense of shock. There had been warm comfort in the thought that Griff must now know the truth. And she had looked forward to hearing him admit he had been wrong about her. She had been waiting for him to instigate yet another truce between them.

'So is that the lot now?' he enquired cheerfully. 'Because if so . . .

'No, that's *not* all!' He needn't think he was going to get round her that quickly.

'I rather thought it wouldn't be.' There was still laughter in his eyes.

'You shouldn't have taken my children without my permission.'

'Admitted,' he took the wind out of her sails by replying, then added insinuatively, 'but it seemed like a good way of getting you up here and it worked, didn't it?'

She was on firmer ground now.

'But that's not fair to *them!* They're beginning to think far too much of you. All I hear, day after day, is Uncle Griff this, Uncle Griff that. They're too young to query your motives.'

'Which are?' His voice was dangerously quiet, sending a frission of chill along her spine. Suddenly the joking was over, but chin tilted she faced him courageously.

'You think I'm fair game, don't you,' she flung at him, 'for a flirtatious affair?'

'Only a *flirtatious* one?' There was still a threatening note in his voice and the way he was shifting his stance as though he found it difficult to remain still was making her increasingly nervous, made her rush into speech once more.

'How do I know how far you expect to . . .?'

'Oh, but you've just implied that you do know!'

'Anyway,' she said hastily, 'that's not all of it. There's the matter of the churchyard. I wasn't going to . . .'

'The churchyard?' He actually sounded bewildered now. 'What possible grievance could you hold against me in connection with that? I confess I'm all agog to hear that one.'

Sandra opened her mouth to tell him, but the sound of someone knocking on the library door prevented her from doing so. With a swift movement Griff inserted the key, turned it and opened the door all in one fluid movement so that no one on the far side could have suspected it of being secured.

'Bradshaw! Everything all right? Had a good time, twins?'

Above their chorused 'yes' the farm manager said wryly,

'Yes, sir. We've brushed 'em down and washed faces and hands.' With a rueful grin at Sandra, 'I'm afraid they got rather mucky, ma'am.'

'See who's come to join us for lunch! Your Mum!'

Griff ushered the twins into the room, ruffling their hair as he did so. It was a natural spontaneous act such as a father might have bestowed, Sandra thought, with a sudden inexplicable stab of pain.

But no—it wasn't inexplicable. As Griff moved towards her smiling and put an arm about her shoulders Sandra knew exactly what ailed her. She would have known it long before if she had been thinking straight. She had been so busy telling herself that Griff could never fit her specification for a husband and father that she had missed an essential factor. Somewhere between their first meeting and this moment, against her will—unsuitable or not—she had fallen in love with Griff Faversham. But what a moment to realise it! She had to get away before she betrayed herself.

'I won't be staying for lunch,' she said hastily. 'The twins can stay—this time. I wouldn't want to disappoint them. But I must get back to Amber. I can't leave her on her own.' It was beside the point that by now Dorian would be home.

Griff followed her out to her car, politely solicitous, the attentive host speeding the parting guest.

'Well, Sandra,' he said, mockingly contemplative, 'I don't know why, but it seems this time we didn't succeed in burying the hatchet.'

If only he knew! But no, it was just as well he didn't. Sandra scarcely remembered the drive back to the village and her thoughts still preoccupied her as she entered the vicarage kitchen.

'That was quick!' Amber looked up from the salad she was preparing. 'I thought you'd be lunching out.' She looked expectantly beyond Sandra. 'The twins not with you?'

'No. They're having lunch with Griff.' And,

defensively, as Amber laughed, 'Just this once.'

'Oh, come on, Sandra! I knew you wouldn't be able to resist his charm,' she teased.

Sandra flushed.

'It wasn't easy,' she confessed in a low voice as she set the table for three.

'Really?' Amber's face lit up. 'Oh, Sandra, does that mean . . .? Oh, it would be marvellous if you married Griff. Then you and the twins need never go away. We'd be neighbours.'

'Thank you,' Sandra smiled wryly. 'It's nice to know you feel that way. But don't get carried away, Amber. I keep telling you, there's no likelihood of me marrying him.'

'But he fancies you, doesn't he?' Amber was bewildered. 'And you've as good as admitted that you fancy him.'

'Yes,' Sandra sighed. 'I do. But I don't want to. Fancying someone and being in love don't always amount to the same thing. And they don't always mean a man would make a good husband and father.'

'It seems to me,' Amber said with a youthful profundity that Sandra found amusing, 'that you're looking for the impossible. Men don't come made to measure, you know.'

'True,' Sandra admitted, 'but if you've made the wrong choice once, as I have, you try not to make the same mistake again. Anyway,' a little irritably, 'this is all theoretical. Griff would probably be horrified if he thought we were weighing him up as husband material. For goodness' sake, let's talk about something else. I noticed as I came past they've nearly finished work on the churchyard.'

'So Dorian said. He's really pleased and very grateful to Griff. Griff's even offered to have repairs done to the roof as well, to stop the altar wall getting damp. Oh, I nearly forgot. While you were up at the Manor, some man phoned. He'd like you to ring back. I can't remember his name but I wrote down the number on the message pad.'

When Sandra returned to the kitchen, Amber and Dorian were waiting lunch for her.

'Sorry,' she said a little abstractedly. 'The call took longer than I expected.'

'Not bad news, was it?' Dorian asked. 'You look a bit worried.'

'Not worried,' Sandra said, 'just exasperated with myself. Well, thank God I didn't open my big mouth and put my foot in it this time.' And as Dorian and Amber waited expectantly, 'Oh, you may as well know. It *was* Griff who arranged for the churchyard to be done.' And as they showed no surprise she explained, 'I thought Crosthwaites over at Filberton were doing it. I asked them to and I thought Griff was claiming the credit. Not that I would have wanted any credit,' she added hastily, 'but it just got my goat to think that he . . . And now,' she sighed, 'I find I've done him yet another injustice. Well, at least I didn't get a chance to say anything and make a fool of myself.' She played listlessly with the salad Amber had placed before her.

'Sandra thinks she's in love with Griff,' Amber told Dorian, 'but she does't think she ought to be.'

'Amber!' Dorian and Sandra remonstrated in unison.

'I'm not sure you should have told me,' Dorian went on, 'not if that was a confidence.' He looked at Sandra. 'But since Amber has let the cat out of the bag, I must say I don't think you could do better than marry Griff Faversham. He . . .'

'He hasn't asked me to,' Sandra emphasised. 'For goodness' sake don't go saying anything to him, either of you.'

'Wouldn't it be marvellous,' Amber enthused, 'if Griff and Sandra could be the first couple to have their wedding photos taken in your new-look churchyard?'

'Personally, I should be delighted,' Dorian agreed. 'But it seems you're being a little premature, my dear.' He looked at Sandra again, his pleasant face concerned for her. 'Do you want to talk about it?'

'In your capacity as vicar?' Sandra's eyes twinkled, though her smile was wry.

'If you like, but in any case as your very good friend. We owe you a lot, Amber and I. We shall miss you when you go. Which reminds me, I hadn't mentioned it as yet, but we'll be getting the compensation money for Amber's accident in a week or two. It will pay for the downstairs alterations and there'll still be some left over. So I've arranged for a young girl to come in on a regular basis as a sort of Girl Friday, to help out with housework and shopping. She's a rather timid school-leaver who isn't keen on seeking employment through the normal channels. So this would be an ideal start for her.'

'I see.' It dawned on Sandra with a sense of shock that she hadn't made any arrangements beyond those necessary to move herself and the twins from London to Vicar's Oak. If she wasn't going to be needed here any more she would have to start house-hunting, she told the Hartochs.

'Good heavens, there's no rush,' Dorian said. 'You're welcome to stay on here as long as you like.'

But Sandra shook her head.

'No, now you two have yourselves sorted out, you

don't need someone living in. You want your privacy. Would it be all right if I left the twins here for a day or so? There's some rather nice property not far from my parents' home that I . . .'

'By all means leave the twins,' Dorian agreed. 'It would be a pity to uproot them before the end of term in any case. If you let me know which day you're going and for how long, I'll arrange for young Elly to come in. She's free any time. She left school at Easter.'

'In that case,' Sandra said slowly, 'how about tomorrow? I think the sooner the better. The longer the twins are here the harder it will be for them to move again.'

Leaving Kent would be a wrench for her as well as for the twins, Sandra realised as she set out next morning. She had come to love the countryside around Vicar's Oak. She liked the life of the small village and the people who inhabited it. But it hadn't been just the twins she had been considering when she had spoken of making a quick clean break. The sooner she was away from Griff Faversham's environment, the easier it would be to put him out of her mind.

Sandra spent four or five days looking at properties. There were several delightful cottages well within her price range, but somehow she couldn't seem to make up her mind or feel enthusiasm for any of them.

'You certainly don't want to rush into anything,' her father advised when she confided in him. 'Buying a house is almost as serious a proposition as getting married,' he teased. 'Why not leave a final decision until you've made the break with Nonie's family and got back here? You know your mother and I would be delighted to put you up meanwhile.'

'Perhaps you're right,' Sandra conceded. 'I'll take

the estate agents' brochures back with me and show them to the twins. It's going to be their home too. So they ought to have a say in the choice.'

The drive back to Vicar's Oak took Sandra far less time than on the first occasion. The last five miles, from the hop fields to the vicarage, seemed almost like coming home, and she found herself looking out for a Land Rover driven by a tall man with glinting coppery hair.

Very unusually, the back door to the vicarage was locked. Knocking at the front did not produce any results, and it had never seemed necessary during her stay at Vicar's Oak to ask for a key. It was true she hadn't let anyone know she was returning today but she would have expected to find someone in. It wasn't even the day Dorian took Amber to Dartford to visit her grandmother. But what about the twins? They should have been home from school an hour since. Sandra began to worry. There were so many horrific stories these days about children going missing between school and home. Dorian had promised faithfully that he himself would take them in the morning and collect them every afternoon.

Sandra was hovering by her car wondering what to do when the curtains at a front window twitched and she saw a thin childish face looking at her. Then the window opened a fraction and she saw the watcher was a girl of sixteen or so.

'Wh-what do you want? The Vicar said I needn't open the door to nobody.' This must be Dorian's nervous Girl Friday, Sandra decided.

'I'm Mrs Tyler, Mrs Hartoch's friend. I'm staying here,' she explained.

'The twins' mother?' the girl asked and as Sandra nodded, 'They're stoppin' at the Manor with Mr

Faversham now. I've got jobs to do. And the Reverend said I needn't open the door for no one,' she repeated. The window closed before Sandra could protest.

Damn, damn, damn! What was going on? Where were Dorian and Amber? And how on earth did Anna and Leo come to be staying at the Manor? Reluctantly she concluded there was only one way to find out.

Sandra hadn't expected to be visiting the Manor again, she thought, as she braked, cautiously this time, on the gravel forefront. Meredith, who answered the door as usual, said that Master Leo and Miss Anna were taking tea with Mr Griff and that he was certain Mrs Tyler could go straight through.

She had arrived just in the midst of a disaster, Sandra discovered. Young Polly Bradshaw, the parlourmaid, was in the process of scraping jam from one of Molly Faversham's priceless Aubusson rugs, while a guilt-ridden Leo looked on.

'Children didn't ought to be allowed to eat in here, sir,' the maid was saying to Griff as Sandra entered, and Sandra quite agreed. This was just the kind of eventuality she had foreseen. Leo took one look at his mother and hurled himself into her arms.

'I didn't do it on purpose,' he howled.

'Of course you didn't, love,' she agreed, then, 'What's going on, Griff? Why are the twins here. The girl at the vicarage said they were staying here.'

'That's right,' Griff told her cheerfully. 'No one knew when to expect you back. None of us knew your parents' telephone number. So when Dorian and Amber had to rush off, it seemed best to bring the twins here.'

'Rush off?' Sandra asked, filled with anxiety. 'Why, is something wrong?'

'No,' Griff said reasurringly, 'if anything it's probably good news. A day or two after you left, Amber started getting tingling sensations in her legs. Then, yesterday morning, she suddenly moved her right foot. Dorian telephoned the specialist and he said to take her in right away for an examination.'

'Oh, how marvellous!' Sandra said. She felt tears welling up in her eyes. 'Oh, I do hope . . .' She stopped as a thought occurred. 'But that means the twins slept *here* last night?'

'Yes,' Anna interrupted importantly, 'and we're sleeping here again tonight and every night until Auntie Amber comes back.'

'We're in the nursery room,' Leo volunteered. 'It used to be Uncle Griff's. There's a fort and a rocking horse . . .'

'And a gi-normous doll's house . . .' Anna put in.

'That was my mother's not mine, I hasten to add,' Griff put in humorously.

'We *can* stay, can't we, Mummy?' Leo pleaded, reading his mother's doubtful expression.

'I suppose you'll have to,' Sandra said slowly. 'The vicarage is all locked up and somehow I don't think Elly whatever-her-name-is will let us in.'

'That means you'll have to stay too, Mummy,' Anna declared. 'Shall I help you choose a room? There are lots and lots of bedrooms in this house.'

'Oh, no,' Sandra said hastily, 'I can't do that. I'll drive into Godmersham and . . .'

'You most certainly won't,' Griff interrupted positively. 'You can perfectly well stay here.' And as she parted her lips for further protest, 'I'm sure a household of staff provides adequate chaperonage, if that's what's worrying you.'

'It's not,' she lied.

'Well then?'

'Well, perhaps I could stay here just for tonight then,' she said awkwardly. 'Thank you.'

'Not at all!' His tone was dry. 'I do realise what an ordeal it must be for you to find yourself and your children under my roof.'

'Have you been behaving yourselves?' she asked the twins hastily.

'They've been excellent,' Griff answered for them.

'We like it here, Mummy,' Anna said. 'Come and see our rooms, Mummy,' she begged.

'Rooms?' Sandra queried as she allowed herself to be dragged up two flights of stairs.

'We have a room each, one on either side of the playroom,' Anna said.

'Uncle Griff said that boys should have their own rooms.' Leo didn't sound too certain about the idea. He and Anna had always shared. Sandra had known the time was coming when they would have to be separated, but in view of Leo's traumas since Geoffrey's death she had postponed the event. Still it was a bit much, she thought, that Griff should take it upon himself to make the decision.

It was strange to be spending the evening at the Manor knowing that the twins were upstairs in bed. Griff had excused himself after dinner. He had, he said, to go over to the Bradshaws' estate cottage to get a report from his farm manager on the last two days.

'I drove the Hartochs up to London,' he explained. 'I thought the car would be better for Amber than travelling all the way by train. And I only got back this afternoon. I shouldn't be too long,' he promised, 'and then we can talk.'

The television was on in the drawing-room but Sandra found herself unable to concentrate on the flickering images as she waited for Griff's return. She was nervous of being alone with him in case anything he said or did caused her to betray her feelings for him.

At last she could bear the tension no longer. She consulted her watch. It wasn't an unreasonably early hour to go to bed after the long drive she had had. She could escape upstairs before Griff returned. But she had left it a little too late. As she rose from her chair and moved towards the door of the drawing-room he entered. With a falsely bright smile she said,

'I'd no idea it was so late. I think I'll go up.' She began to move towards the door. Then her smile froze.

'Oh, not yet Sandra, surely. We haven't had our talk.' Without making his action seem deliberate, he had contrived to place himself between Sandra and the door.

'But you told me all you know about Amber over dinner. And I am very tired. I've had a long drive today.'

'I've driven quite a way myself,' he observed. He yawned and stretched and, unwillingly fascinated, Sandra saw the play of powerful muscles beneath the tautened material of his shirt. 'I was looking forward to a relaxing chat over a drink. Won't you join me in something?'

'No, thank you. All I need now is sleep. Once I've looked in on the twins, I . . .'

'And for some reason,' he said astutely, 'you're very anxious not to be left alone with me. And yet I thought we had some unfinished business. Last time I saw you—correct me if I'm wrong—we were just about to discuss the churchyard, wasn't it? You were about to tell me what crime I'd committed in that direction.'

'You hadn't,' she said quickly. 'It was a mistake, a misunderstanding. I . . .'

'Yet another misunderstanding?' A smile lurked at the corners of his mouth. 'I must be the most misunderstood man of your acquaintance. Or do you make a habit of leaping to conclusions where my sex is concerned?'

'No,' indignantly, 'I don't. It was just unfortunate that . . .'

'Then may I take it you no longer have any quarrel with me?'

'Yes. That is, no. I mean . . .' Sandra was confused and at her incoherent speech he lifted an inquisitorial eyebrow.

'I think that means we have yet another truce? Yes?'

'Griff, I really am tired. I can't think straight.' But her inability to concentrate owed more to his proximity than to fatigue.

'You never did tell me,' he went on, ignoring her remark, 'just how you feel about me—when we're not in the midst of a misunderstanding, that is.'

'I . . .' She backed a step or two. This was just what she didn't want to discuss.

'Because, on occasions, I've had the distinct impression that you feel about me the way I feel about you. Hmm?'

'Since I don't know how you . . . I mean, I don't . . .'

'Then perhaps it's time I told you.' He took a step in her direction and immediately she felt her blood-pressure soar. 'Sandra, I . . . what the . . .?'

Another hasty retreat had brought the back of her knees into contact with one of the Chippendale sofas and she toppled backward, just as Meredith entered carrying a small tray. Politely the stately butler averted his eyes from the sight of long shapely legs and the visible flounce of dainty lingerie.

'I thought you might be in need of some refreshment before retiring, sir.'

As the butler placed the tray on a small table, Sandra scrambled to her feet, taking advantage of his presence to make her escape. She hurried from the room with a hasty goodnight, directed impartially between both men, not daring to meet Griff's eye as she spoke.

CHAPTER EIGHT

THE twins were sound asleep. Anna as always was tidy and composed, her small face serene. Leo was curled in a tight ball. His bedclothes had fallen to the floor, and in one hand he clutched a wooden soldier from the fort. Gently Sandra replaced the covers and stood watching him for a while, her heart full of tenderness. Whatever happened, she always had the twins. Their love for her and hers for them should be sufficient happiness.

Occasionally Leo's face worked convulsively, as though his dreams troubled him, and she sighed. He had been sleeping much better since they'd moved to the country. He liked the little school he and Anna attended. He had grown fond of the family at the vicarage. She hoped another move wouldn't undo all that living in Vicar's Oak had accomplished for him. For Leo's sake mainly she would have to introduce the subject carefully.

In the bedroom allocated to her Sandra found her fatigue had vanished. She had been right to avoid a *tête-a-tête* with Griff, but she felt restless and edgy. Not even the nightly ritual of removing make-up and brushing her brown hair until it shone could soothe her ragged nerve-ends. Nor could she prevent herself from wondering what Griff might have said if he hadn't been interrupted.

Undressed and ready for bed, she looked around for something to read, but none of the books on the bedside shelf appealed to her and there was no way she was going to venture out of this room in search of something more compelling. With a sigh she extinguished the bedside lamp, curled herself up in much the same attitude as her son had adopted, and willed herself to sleep.

She must have succeeded, for it was from heavy depths of slumber that she struggled up when the screaming began. But once she was awake it did not take her long to recognise the sound and its source.

'Oh, no! Leo!' She leapt out of bed and in too much of a hurry to put on a wrap she ran barefoot along the landing and up the next flight of stairs.

By the dim light of the lamp which Leo must always have while he slept, she could see the small boy sitting bolt upright in bed. His eyes were still closed, but his clenched fists flailed the air and he was still emitting the ear-splitting noise that had woken her.

'Mummy's here, darling, Mummy's here. It's all right, Leo!'

Sandra bent and gathered him into her arms, murmuring soothing endearments, but the small body remained rigid. Leo's blond hair was darkened and his pyjamas soaked with perspiration.

'What the hell's going on? I thought someone was being murdered.'

Sandra, her arms still wrapped about her son, looked up to see Griff in the doorway clad in pyjama bottoms, a towelling robe falling open to expose a broad expanse of bare chest.

'Ssh!' she cautioned him. 'Don't shout. He mustn't be woken suddenly.'

Griff moved towards the bed.

'Nightmare?' he asked softly. His expression was sympathetic. 'Gerry used to suffer with them. Here, let me.' Before Sandra could realise what he was doing, he had detached Leo from her arms. He wrapped the shuddering child in a blanket and sat down in a large armchair with him. 'Shut the door or he'll wake Anna,' he commanded and Sandra found herself obeying him. 'Leo, Leo,' he repeated the boy's name quietly but insistently, 'wake up now. It's all right.'

After a few seconds the dreadful screaming stopped, but Leo was sobbing now, a tearing sound that held fear and wrung Sandra's heart strings.

'Daddy? Daddy, I didn't mean it.'

Over the boy's head, Griff's eyes met Sandra's questioningly.

'Do you know what he's talking about?' he murmured.

Puzzled, she shook her head.

'I suppose it might have something to do with the accident with the jam, this afternoon. He's always been a bit accident-prone and Geoffrey used to shout at him if he made a mess at table.'

Griff grimaced, then said to Leo, 'It's all right, old chap. Come on, now. Wake up and tell Uncle Griff what it's all about.'

Slowly, painfully the child's eyelids fluttered open, almost as if, Sandra thought, there was something he feared to see. His expression lightened a little, then, 'Uncle Griff? Is it really you? I thought . . .'

'Of course it's me! Your Mum's here too. See? Sandra, put the main light on.'

'Mummy?' For the first time in Leo's life he showed reluctance to look at her. Instead he turned his face against Griff's broad chest. 'I'm sorry,' he quavered. 'It wasn't my fault. Don't be cross with me, Mummy.'

Sandra knelt at Griff's feet, forgetting in her concern for her small son that she wore only the most transparent of nightgowns.

'Darling, Mummy's not cross with you. Why ever should she be? You've had a bad dream, that's all. Do you want to talk about it?'

'No. You don't know what I've done,' he sobbed into Griff's shoulder, and further than that he refused to be drawn.

'Suppose you leave us?' Griff suggested to Sandra and as she swiftly shook her head, he said persuasively, 'I think Leo might find it easier to tell *me* what's worrying him. It must surely be something more than a drop of spilt jam.' And gently, as she still hesitated, 'It'll be OK, Sandra. Trust me. Wait for me in the nursery.'

The minutes seemed endless to Sandra as she paced the toy-filled room. She could hear nothing from behind the closed door. To occupy herself she looked in on Anna, but her daughter was sleeping quite undisturbed. What was worrying Leo? she fretted. Children were such a responsibility; until these last few weeks Sandra had not realised quite how much of a responsibility. If there had been traumas in the twins' earlier years, she had not been told about them. Geoffrey had not allowed her much time for visiting the nursery and there had always been Nanny. She still had a lot to learn, Sandra realised. So what was she doing out here while Griff Faversham comforted her son? She took an impatient step towards the bedroom door just as it opened and Griff emerged. He set one finger on his lips and with his other hand took her arm, urging her out on to the landing.

'He's all right now. He's fast asleep. And you're cold.' For the first time he seemed to notice her state of undress, and immediately Sandra herself was conscious of thin material, a plunging V-neck and lacy cups emphasising her breasts which did not disguise the darkened aureoles and the nipples at their centres.

Defensively she folded her arms across her breasts, but at that moment she was still more concerned about her son.

'Leo? Are you sure he's all right? Did he tell you . . .? You should have let me . . .'

'Yes, he told me. And I'll tell you. But first . . . Here, put this on.' He pulled off his towelling robe and enveloped her in it. It was far too big for her and it still held the warmth of his body, the scent of him; and it was strangely comforting as was his arm about her shoulders. He urged her towards her room, but on the threshold she stopped.

'Leo . . .?' she began.

With a little exclamation of impatience Griff bent and scooped her up. He tucked her into bed pulling the covers around her as impersonally as her father might have done. But Sandra shivered, and not from the cold this time.

'Leo,' Griff told her somewhat grimly, 'has been suffering from the delusion that his father's death was his fault.'

'What?'

'Had you no idea?' To her sensitive ears he sounded accusing.

'No!' Sandra was shocked. 'I hadn't. But why on earth should he?'

'You and your husband had rows in front of the children?'

'Not if I could help it. But it wasn't always possible . . .'

'Leo adores you. You know that?' He sat down on the edge of the bed.

'Yes.' There was something in Griff's eyes Sandra could not quite fathom and she lowered hers, picked nervously at the bedclothes. 'Geoffrey always said he clung too much.'

'Because Leo loves you and hated hearing your quarrels, he told his father he wished he were dead.'

'He actually told Geoffrey that?' Sandra wouldn't have believed Leo capable of such temerity where his father was concerned.

'Apparently so, and the next day your husband was killed in the car crash. Leo felt responsible. It's worried him ever since.'

Sandra's eyes filled with tears and her mouth quivered.

'Oh, the poor darling.' She thrust aside the covers in an attempt to get out of bed. ' I must go to him.' But gently Griff restrained her.

'He's all right, Sandra. He's asleep. We had a long talk and I was able to reassure him. I told him things didn't happen in that way and that you would say exactly the same thing—that in no way was he to blame for his father's accident.'

'Do you think he believed you?' Sandra asked anxiously. Her instincts were still to go to her son.

'Yes. But if necessary we must go on saying it. He's been a very unhappy little boy.'

'I really had no idea.' Sandra was swamped with guilt and a feeling of inadequacy. How could she not have realised how deeply her own child was troubled? She was still on the verge of tears herself. 'If only I'd known . . .'

'If you had,' Griff said soothingly, 'you would have comforted him as I did, of course you would. And whatever you do,' he said perceptively, 'don't go blaming yourself.' He put a hand over hers. 'Right now I think you could do with a little comforting yourself.' Huskily, 'Sandra, won't you let me be the one to comfort you too?'

Sandra's tear-filled eyes met his and she found herself unable to look away. There was something in his face which made her want to throw herself into his arms, to lean on his strength as Leo had done. But she was in a highly emotional state just now. It was dangerous to be ruled by emotions. She tried to free her hand, blinked away the traitorous tears.

'I'm . . . I'm all right,' she told him with a courageous lift of her chin. 'Thank you for helping Leo. Goodnight, Griff.' But he ignored the dismissal.

'Sandra!' Only her name said in a throaty voice. Just a tightening of the fingers that held her hand. But Sandra found she was trembling. She wished Griff would go away before the surging need she felt to be held and caressed totally submerged her. She couldn't help noticing how large and strong his hands were. And if she raised her eyes she would see the broad, bare chest with its bronzed curly hair a shade lighter than his head. She could imagine only too well how its texture would feel beneath exploring fingers.

'You'd better have your dressing-gown back,' she told him, another hint that he should leave.

'Only if *I* can take it off,' he murmured. 'Sandra,' he gave a sharp intake of breath, 'I want to make love to you, you know that, don't you?'

'Oh, no!' She fought harder for the possession of her hand, but he was using it to pull her closer and then she was in his arms, pressed against his bare torso. His mouth had opened fiercely over hers and she murmured something incoherent as she felt the warmth of him through the material of her nightdress. Both of her hands were free now, free to stroke the firm contours of his back. His mouth on hers grew more avid. His breathing was faster and shallower. 'Griff,' she protested feebly as he pushed away the bedclothes that separated them and his exploring fingers found the smooth contour of her hip. 'Griff, don't, please . . . I . . .'

'I want to be closer to you, Sandra, much closer,' he breathed. 'I want to lie there beside you, hold you in my arms. I want to touch you, have you touch me.' His hand curved around her buttocks and he strained her to him making her aware of his hardened desire.

Tremor after tremor of responsive need racked her body and though some small, still sane part of her knew this was madness her mouth sought his, her lips parting moistly, her tongue parrying then mimicking the invasion of his.

'Are you kissing my Mummy goodnight?' a voice asked interestedly.

'Oh, God!' Sandra heard Griff breathe. 'Such are the penalties of being a parent!'

The sound of Anna's voice and Griff's impatient words restored Sandra's sense of proportion. But there was no need to push him away. He was already on his feet.

'Anna?' Sandra knew her voice sounded shaky. 'What are you doing out of bed?' It was most unusual for her daughter to wake in the night.

'I've got a sore throat.'

At once Sandra was all mother, the languor induced by Griff's lovemaking shaken off. She slid from the bed, pulling Griff's robe around her.

'Mummy's coming, darling. We'll soon make it better.'

'Pop back to the nursery, there's a good girl,' Griff suggested. 'Your mother will be with you in a minute.'

'I'm coming right now,' Sandra said reassuringly as Anna hovered anxiously.

'Sandra,' Griff put a detaining hand on her arm,' I have to talk to you.'

'Not now, Griff, please. Anna needs me.'

'I realise that, dammit, but so do I,' he muttered *sotto voce* for her ears only. 'I'll wait here for you.'

'No, don't,' she said hastily. 'I've no idea how long I'll be.' Anna's unexpected arrival had saved her from making a dreadful mistake.

'However long it takes, I'll be waiting, right here,' he insisted as she took Anna's hand and led her from the room. 'And don't think you can get out of it by staying up there. I shall come and fetch you.'

Sandra knew Griff was quite capable of carrying out that threat. But even after Anna was settled she loitered. Part of her longed to be in his arms again, knowing the thrill of his kisses, his caresses. Part of her was unwilling to face whatever confrontation he had in mind. When someone said they wanted to talk, she had discovered in the past, it could turn out to be an uncomfortable experience. She peeped in at Leo, but he was sleeping soundly and at last she nerved herself to go downstairs.

Griff was lying on her bed and at first she thought he had fallen asleep. But as he turned his head to look at her she saw there was nothing relaxed about him.

'Everything all right?' he asked and as she nodded. 'Good!' He sat up and swung his long legs over the side of the bed. 'Perhaps now we can have some time to ourselves. Come here.'

But Sandra shook her head.

'Griff, I think you ought to go now. It's late and . . .'

'Precisely.' He stood up and moved towards her. He

didn't touch her but just his proximity was exciting. 'Late at night seems to be our only chance of being alone, of talking without interruption.' Wryly, he added, 'Or so I thought.'

'There isn't anything to talk about,' she protested uneasily. It wasn't just conversation for which she felt reluctant, but what being alone with Griff might lead to, the sensations his nearness could stir in the deep, dark, most intimate places of her being.

'We *have* to talk about us,' he insisted. 'No, don't say anything. Just hear me out. Come and sit down.' He held out a hand to her and indicated the bed.

Sandra ignored the hand and sat instead in a small basket chair safely distanced from him.

'All right. I'll listen,' she sighed, 'but only because I can't physically *make* you go!'

With a resigned expression on his face he sat down on the edge of the bed.

'I did it again, didn't I? I went too fast for you? But it's damned difficult, Sandra, not to . . . when I . . . Sandra,' huskily, 'I *want* you. I think I've wanted you since the first moment I clapped eyes on you.'

She shifted uneasily in the chair.

'Griff, I think you should know . . .'

'You said you'd hear me out,' he reminded her. 'I tried slowing the pace, because I could tell you weren't the kind to be rushed. But even that didn't seem to suit you. You refused to go out with me, refused to give yourself a chance to get to know me. Why, Sandra?'

She spread her hands in a helpless gesture. She couldn't very well tell him she had been afraid of the attraction he held for her, that she hadn't wanted to give way to it, in case she fell in love with him; that anyone with whom she fell in love would have to measure up to certain standards.

'At first,' he said, 'I thought you were interested in Dorian. Both my mother and Nonie were always saying what a marvellous wife you would have made him. I was disappointed in you and—yes—I was as jealous as hell. But instead you seem to have been instrumental in bringing him and his wife together again.' A little doubtfully, 'You are happy about that, aren't you Sandra?'

'Yes,' she told him vehemently, 'yes, of course,' and saw his satisfied nod.

'Initially we were at odds, you and I. You thought me unfeeling where Amber was concerned. And I suppose I was. But I'm only human. There was my mother's heartbreak to contend with. I had lost a brother, and you can't blame me for that more than I blame myself.'

'But I *don't* blame you!' Sandra felt compelled to interrupt. She went on earnestly, 'And *you* mustn't go on torturing yourself about Gerry's death. It was an accident. It might easily have happened anyway, later if not then.'

'Sandra!' He held out a hand to her again, his voice pleading, 'Come here to me,' and as she shook her head, 'I just want to hold you, to have you near me while we talk. I swear I won't do anything you don't want me to do.'

The trouble was, when she was near him, she wanted him to kiss and caress her, and she wouldn't be able to hide that fact. She remained where she was.

'You've done so much good, to so many people, in the short time you've been here. Amber, Dorian, Nonie, my mother. They're all better for your having been here. I only want to share in the happiness you've brought everyone else,' he coaxed. 'Is that too much to ask?'

She swallowed convulsively. It wasn't fair of him to appeal to her emotions like this, to her generous impulses. However much he might need comfort, she wasn't going to start an affair with Griff Faversham.

'When we were in London, Dorian told me about the churchyard, that you'd planned to have it landscaped for him. I'm sorry if I trod on your toes over that.'

'You didn't!' Sandra exclaimed. 'It wasn't that. So long as it was done who arranged it wasn't important. It was just that . . .' But she wasn't given a chance to finish.

'Then what does matter to you, Sandra?' He sounded baffled. 'It isn't the accident, it isn't Dorian or the churchyard. So what is it? Do I repulse you? I didn't think I . . .'

'No, Griff,' honesty compelled her to admit, 'it's none of those things. I . . .'

'Then *what*, for God's sake?' It was as if he could no longer sit still, but came to stand beside her, towering over her. A restlessness emanated from him. 'Just tell me, Sandra! Make me understand.'

'I can't.' She stared down fixedly at her hands clenched in her lap. She still had his robe on, she noted absently, while he still wore only his pyjama bottoms. To her heightened senses his body seemed to exude a heat that reached out and encompassed her in its aura. She wanted to be drawn further into it.

'I'll make you tell me!' He reached down and hauled her to her feet, held her hard up against him and as their bodies melded she felt his rising tautness and exquisite sensation stabbed through her.

'Griff,' she implored, but his hands were caressing her body, touching, arousing, destroying her resistance.

He unfastened the robe she wore, his hands warm and insistent on the taut contours of her breasts, his fingers moving across and around their jutting peaks, until she felt faint with sensation. Despite herself she shuddered, pressing into him.

'God, Sandra,' he muttered, 'why not admit it? You want me, as much as I want you. You can't deny it.' He didn't wait for her answer, but covered her face with kisses, his tongue invading the inner softness of her mouth. She was conscious of nothing but his nearness, of his wanting, of her own aching need. Her hands found their own way around his neck and though she knew it was madness she arched her body to his even more urgently.

With a sudden movement that caught her off balance he swung her into his arms and carried her over to the bed. He slid his robe from her shoulders then laid her down, joined her there. He pushed down the thin straps of her nightdress, kissing each shoulder in turn. With seeking mouth and fingers he roused her while she in turn explored his body, unable to deny herself the tactile pleasure of knowing its strength and hardness.

'Sandra,' he groaned, 'I want to be closer to you, the greatest closeness a man and a woman can achieve. Let me love you,' he urged, 'let me love you now! Say you'll marry me.'

She went still suddenly under his hands.

'Wh-what did you say?' she asked incredulously.

'I love you, Sandra. I want to marry you.'

She pulled away from him, sat up.

'I didn't know you wanted . . . I thought . . .'

'Good grief, Sandra!' He rolled on to his back, stared up at her. 'What did you think this was all about?'

'I thought,' she said slowly, 'you just wanted an affair with me.'

'And you'd have gone along with that?' He actually sounded shocked.

'No!' she said indignantly. 'Of course I wouldn't. I don't . . .'

'But another minute and we'd have been making love. You know we would.'

'No,' she said again a little wildly, 'I wouldn't have let it go that far. I *wouldn't* . . .'

'You mean you'd have led me on just so far and then . . .?'

'No! I'm not like that.' She was appalled to have given him that idea. 'I . . . Oh God, I can't *think!*' She jumped up and walked to the window, rested her forehead against the cool panes. 'I didn't mean to let you go so far and I didn't know,' she said again, 'that you wanted to marry me. But it doesn't make any difference.' Despair sounded in her voice. 'I can't marry you, Griff.'

She heard the thud as his feet hit the floor and next moment he was behind her, his hands on her bare shoulders.

'And I can't, *won't* accept that. You tell me you've no further grievance against me. Every reaction of your body tells me you want me. So give me one good reason why . . .'

'Let go of me,' she begged in strangled tones, 'and I'll give you several.'

'No!' He spun her round to face him. 'You're going to look me in the face while you tell me. And I warn you I'm going to take a hell of a lot of convincing. Dammit, Sandra, you *can't* convince me.'

Somehow she managed to meet his eyes.

'All right!' She croaked and had to clear her voice. 'I'm physically attracted to you, of course I am. I can't deny that. But we're not suited in other ways, you and I. I can't marry you because I couldn't live in your world. I'm not lady of the manor material. No,' as he seemed about to speak, 'you made me hear *you* out. Now *you* listen. I was married for several years to an ambitious man, a social climber,' she said with distaste. 'He wanted me to climb with him and I hated every moment of it. It was a false, unreal existence. The people were shallow, insincere. I'm an ordinary person, from an ordinary background, and I just couldn't live up to what he wanted of me. If I marry again I want what my parents have. Simplicity, love that doesn't try to change or dominate.'

'So that's what you meant by position, and I thought . . . I should have known better. You're not the acquisitive sort. Oh Sandra, Sandra,' he sighed, 'I do understand. And *I* don't want to dominate you or to change you. For heaven's sake I love you as you are—*because* you're what you are. Surely you can accept me for the same reasons?' She wished she could. His hands had begun to caress her shoulders but she went on doggedly.

'Geoffrey didn't want children. I did—desperately. I wanted a big family. Still want one. He bitterly resented the two we had. He wouldn't even let me look after them myself. You've seen what that did to Leo. I'd never marry another man who doesn't want a family.'

'For God's sake!' Griff broke out in exasperation. 'What makes you think I don't want children?'

'Things you've said. When we first met you said you didn't want to be lumbered with other people's children. And tonight, when Anna walked in on us, you said . . .'

'Sandra! Sandra!' he groaned. 'Are you going to hold

it against me that I was so frustrated that in my need to make love to you, I resented an interruption—from anyone? Besides, I was afraid my being in your room might upset the child. If we were married I'd have the right to be there. And Leo and Anna aren't anybody's children. They're *yours*, part of you,' throatily, 'as *I* want to be. You accused me once of using them. Perhaps I did, a little. But that wasn't my only motive, my darling. I wanted to get to know them, to have them know me—accept me.'

'But I want to have more children, Griff, as well as the twins. But your life-style would make that impossible.'

'How, for heaven's sake?'

'Children need a home, not a showplace. All those ornaments, antiques, valuable . . .'

'If that's all that's worrying you, we'll put the damned things in the attic.'

'Oh, your mother would love that! All her . . .!'

'My mother will *love* having grandchildren. She adores the twins already. And what do you think she did with the ornaments when Gerry and I were kids?' he demanded. Then huskily, 'I'd like you to have *our* children. In fact I shall insist on it. No, Sandra, you'll have to find more convincing excuses than those not to marry me. You've got the wrong idea about the Favershams, my love.' From her shoulders his hands slid up her neck, beneath the glossy hair, caressed the sensitive nape. 'We don't live in style as you call it, never have. We've always been well off, yes, but that's just the luck of the draw. We're simple folk at heart—farming folk. And I've certainly no social ambitions. I've no time for them. It was Gerry who liked to mix with the county set. The estate, my museum, they're all I've ever wanted,' significantly, 'until now!'

'But you have considered marriage,' Sandra argued. 'You've been engaged before. You said they couldn't live up to your life-style. So how can I?'

Griff laughed indulgently and she knew he sensed she was weakening.

'They couldn't live *down* to it! My unlamented fiancées, my darling Sandra, found me very, very boring. Like you they expected the lord of the manor to live the high life. Unlike you, that was what they wanted. They were disappointed. Now,' masterfully, 'any other objections before I ask you again if you'll marry me?'

Sandra found she couldn't think of even one. Shyly, still doubtful, she looked up at him, shook her head.

'No,' she murmured, felt the blood rush up under her skin. 'I—I would like to marry you, Griff, if you're really sure that's what you want. That I . . .'

'Sure ?' He hugged her tightly and she felt his body stir suddenly against hers. *'I've* been sure for a very long time, my love. But you've led me quite a chase. Not any more, though.' He swooped, picked her up and made as if he would return to the bed with her, but,

'Griff, wait!'

'Oh, no!' With a groan that was only half humorous, he set her on her feet again. 'Don't tell me! You've just remembered some crime of mine we haven't covered.'

CHAPTER NINE

'NO,' Sandra told Griff with a demure twinkle. 'But there's one small thing *you've* overlooked.'

'Which is?' he sighed resignedly.

'You haven't asked me yet if *I* love *you.*'

'Is that all?' He growled mock-ferociously. 'And do you?' The expression on his face, the grip of his hands at her waist dared her to deny it.

'Yes,' she sighed melting against him, 'I do love you, Griff. To be honest I think I must always have loved you, right from the start, but . . .'

'No buts,' he put a finger on her lips, 'and that's enough talking. There are other very satisfactory ways of demonstrating how much you love me.'

'Griff, we're not married yet,' she began as he took her in his arms once more. 'Do you . . .?'

'And being my conventional, don't-rush-me Sandra, I suppose, you would rather I didn't make love to you until we were married.' She sensed the tenseness in him as he waited for her answer.

'I . . .' She broke off as somewhere in the house a telephone began to ring stridently.

'Ignore it,' Griff murmured against her neck, 'Meredith can answer it. You were saying?'

'We can't ignore it,' Sandra said worriedly. 'Meredith's probably asleep. Besides it's a shame to get him up when we're already awake. You'd better answer it.' To her mind the sound of a telephone ringing in the small hours was linked with trouble. It had been the middle of the night when she had heard of Geoffrey's accident.

'OK,' he said resignedly, 'but I'll be back. I've let you get away from me once or twice, but not any more.'

She heard him run downstairs whistling light-heartedly. If the truth were known, she was relieved at this short respite. She needed time to gather her wits, to assimilate all that had happened. She seemed to have promised to marry Griff, she thought wonderingly. But incredulity was followed immediately by a surging joy. It really did seem that Griff embodied all she desired, that he was her man made to measure. She wanted compatibility, stability for herself and the twins. But, she realised, that was not all. For herself she need the earth-shattering excitement of the senses, the fulfilment that his love-making foretold.

Now she could admit how much she wanted him physically. A little thrilling shudder ran through her, for she could still feel his throbbing, wanting hardness against her. She suspected—and at the knowledge another little frisson ran through her—that Griff would not be prepared to wait until they were married before he made love to her. And she knew that if the telephone had not interrupted her she would have told him that, all her misgivings resolved, she didn't want to wait either.

Impatient for his return, for a resumption of their lovemaking, she realised just how long he had been gone. She went back on to the landing. The telephone was only in the hall below, but she could hear nothing. Indeed the silence held an unusual quality, almost frightening in its intensity. Suddenly she wanted to see Griff, feel his arms about her, know the reassurance of his love. She began to run.

Downstairs, the hall and drawing-room were empty. Instinct led her to the library, Griff's retreat.

He sat behind his desk. Slumped was a better description of his attitude. Head in hands, he was terrifyingly immobile.

'Griff?' Barefoot, she padded across the room to his side, put an enquiring hand on his shoulder.

He lifted his face to hers and she took a step backwards, shocked by its ravaged expression. She scarcely recognised him. She had seen him in many moods—angry, amused, sad, but never this devastated.

'Griff, oh, darling,' she put her arms around him, 'what is it?'

He swallowed and she saw the visible effort it cost him to speak.

'That was a message from the cruise company—about my mother. She's had another heart attack. She's dead.' The words came baldly, starkly, but Sandra recognised the depth of emotion that lay beneath them.

'Oh, my love, my dear, dear love,' she whispered. Her eyes filled with sympathetic tears and she moved closer, cradled his head against her breast. For an instant his arms went about her tightly, painfully. Then as abruptly he released her, rose stiffly, wearily, like an old man.

'I'm going to bed. I'll have to be up early. There'll be arrangements to make.' His voice cracked for an instant. 'I can't quite take it in yet, Sandra. I know no one's immortal. I knew she wasn't well. But to lose her so soon after Gerry. Not to be able to say goodbye, even.' He banged his fist savagely on the desk top. 'I should never have persuaded her to take that cruise. If I hadn't she might have been alive now.'

'Griff, you mustn't think like that. You mustn't always blame yourself for the things that happen. Besides it wasn't just your idea. Her doctor suggested it. Oh, Griff!' Sandra took his hand and for an instant her cheek rested against his bare shoulder. 'I'm so sorry.'

'Thank God I have you now,' he said gruffly.

'Always,' she whispered. 'I'll always be here, Griff.'

Arms around each other they went slowly upstairs. On the landing outside her bedroom door, he stood motionless for an instant. She looked up wonderingly at him, longing to ease his hurt by her loving. With a sudden fierce movement he caught her to him, kissed her—a long, deep, solace-seeking kiss. Then he turned on his heel and a moment later his door slammed.

Slowly she went into her room and got back into bed. The clock on the side table showed only three o'clock. And yet so much had been crammed into these few short hours. She knew it would be impossible for her to sleep now. Her eyes filled with tears again as she thought of Molly Faversham dying so far from home. Poor Nonie must be in a dreadful state too. But most of all she agonised over Griff, grieving now on his own. Her heart ached to be able to hold him in her arms and comfort him. Why shouldn't she go to him and do just that?

The thought had her out of bed and along the landing to his door before she paused doubtfully. Perhaps he wouldn't want her with him at this moment. Perhaps he wanted to grieve in private. She didn't know him well enough to know whether he would consider her presence an intrusion. Yet she knew if she didn't go to him she would always wonder if she had let him down in his need.

With a trembling hand she opened the door, nerved

herself to go in. The room was dark, silent. Only a sliver of moonlight filtering through the curtains showed her the position of the bed. She tiptoed closer, listened for the sound of the steady breathing that would tell her he slept. She heard nothing.

'Griff?' she breathed his name.

'Sandra?'

'Did . . . did I wake you?'

'No.' It was said on a heavy sigh. Then once more there was silence.

With a courage she hadn't known she possessed, Sandra lifted a corner of the bedcover and slid in beside him. The pillow beneath her cheek was slightly damp, and with a little murmur of tenderness she moved towards him, put her arms about him. His body was tense.

'Griff, darling, I'm so very very sorry about your mother.' Apologetically, 'I couldn't bear to think of you being on your own. But if you'd rather I went away . . .'

For answer his arms went round her and he pulled her close, and she felt the swift rise and fall of his chest against her breast.

'Will you stay with me, Sandra? All night?'

'If you want me to,' she said simply.

He made a little sound that was half assent, half contentment, and she felt him relax into her arms.

She lay there possessed by a strange, yearning tenderness she had never known before, at least not for any man. The nearest sensation she had known to this was the love she gave to her children when they were unhappy or hurt. Geoffrey had never had any need of this kind of loving. His demands upon her had been purely physical, leaving her bodily satisfied but still strangely unfulfilled.

After a while Griff's deepened breathing told her that he slept, and she was quite content that it should be so. This wasn't the moment for selfish gratification of sexual desires. It was enough that he needed her close to him. This giving was a part of the deeper love that would grow between them through the years to come.

She lay awake for a long while, deeply, serenely happy in this knowledge of the future. But she must have slept at last for she was aroused by the drowsy knowledge that someone was repeating her name in a low urgent voice.

'Sandra,' Griff murmured again as she stirred and opened her eyes.

In the half-light of dawn she could see his face as he bent over her and she put up a hand to caress his cheek.

'Griff?' she murmured sleepily, then, more alert, 'What is it?'

'I have to get up now. I'm driving up to London. I don't want you to get up,' he said quickly as she sat up, 'but I did want to say goodbye before I go, to thank you for . . .' His voice quivered, then steadied. 'For last night. You don't know how much it meant to me, to have you here, to be able to hold you, Sandra. When I left you at your door—God knows how I did it—I needed you, desperately, just to hold you, nothing more, I swear. But I couldn't ask that of you. And then, my love, miraculously you came to me. Why, Sandra? Weren't you afraid I might . . .?'

'No, I wasn't afraid,' she said softly. 'I came to you, because I want to share everything in your life, your griefs as well as your joys. I didn't come to you because I wanted you to make love to me. The time wasn't right. We both knew that.'

'But you will be here for me, when I come back? You won't get any more silly ideas about not wanting to marry me?'

'I'll be here,' she told him tenderly. 'But please, let me get up and see you off. No, I insist.'

The hours seemed long after Griff had left, even when the twins were up and about and demanding Sandra's attention. Because of Griff's early departure it had been left to her to break the news of Mrs Faversham's death to the staff, and she did so gently, knowing they would all feel the loss of their much loved employer.

This done the day stretched before her. She had no idea when Griff would be back. Certainly not today. Though there was happiness to come that she hugged to herself, it was overshadowed by Griff's bereavement.

'Let's go down to the vicarage,' she suggested to the twins, 'and see if Elly will let us in this time. I need some more of my clothes and so do you two.'

To pass the time they walked. It was a glorious morning and Sandra grieved that Molly Faversham was no longer alive to enjoy its beauty. On a day such as this the older woman's beloved walled garden was a demi-paradise of scent and colour.

Sandra had been a little worried about telling the twins the sad news, but after a moment of gravity they were behaving quite normally, one moment fast friends, the next squabbling over some trivial matter.

Sandra hadn't a great deal of confidence about gaining admission to the vicarage, so she was surprised when she found the back door unlocked and even more surprised when she walked in to find Dorian rather haphazardly preparing himself some breakfast.

'I didn't know you were back!' she exclaimed as she took over the task. Then, excitedly, 'Is Amber with you? How is she?'

Dorian beamed seraphically. Forsaking his usually grave manner the words tumbled out of him.

'No, she's not here, but she's doing fine. The doctors are very hopeful of a full recovery. But they're keeping her in for a few days, for some tests. I had to come back. I couldn't neglect the parish for too long. And how have you been getting on. Did you find a house?'

'The house of my dreams!' She grinned at him, thinking how surprised he would be when he heard just whose house it was, then, remembering, 'But you won't have heard the bad news?' And as he tilted his head enquiringly, 'About Mrs Faversham?'

Dorian was distressed, naturally, but as a clergyman his mind was almost immediately on the needs of the living.

'Poor Griff. He'll have taken it hard, and so soon after Gerry's death. And then there's Nonie! My goodness,' he exclaimed worriedly, 'she must be in a dreadful state. She'll want to come home immediately of course.'

'Griff has thought of all that,' Sandra assured him. They had discussed it during Griff's preparations for departure. 'He's going to arrange for her to be flown home with . . . with . . .' Her voice broke and Dorian nodded understandingly.

'Let me know as soon as he gets home. I'll come up and see him. That is . . . I suppose you're staying on at the Manor? I mean with Amber and Nonie both away, you can hardly . . .'

'Of course,' she said hastily seeing that he was in danger of entangling himself in embarrassment. 'I would have stayed there anyway.' And then unable to conceal her feelings any longer she told him her news. She couldn't have wished for a more enthusiastic reception.

'I'm very happy for both of you,' Dorian exclaimed. 'And so will Amber be when I tell her. I know she hated the thought of losing you. And having you will make it a little easier for Griff to bear his loss. Have you set a date?' Again the practical clergyman was to the fore. 'Where will you hold the ceremony?' His face fell. 'Of course it's normal to have the wedding at the bride's home church.' Sandra knew exactly what he was thinking.

'We hadn't got around to discussing any details when . . . when we got the telephone message about Mrs Faversham. The wedding won't be for a while now, I should think. It wouldn't seem right so soon after . . .'

In fact it was a month later, when out of respect for Mrs Faversham's memory, Dorian performed a very quiet marriage service. If Sandra's parents were disappointed at not being able to make a big splash in their own locality for their only child, they were tactful enough not to mention it.

'Dorian's over the moon that you want to get married in his church,' a radiant Amber had told Sandra when the arrangements were first mooted. 'He's sure it will encourage other couples to follow suit now that the grounds look so nice. And I'm so thrilled that you've asked me to be your matron of honour. I love my dress, and Anna is going to look really sweet in hers.'

Amber could walk a little now with the aid of two sticks, and was determined that on the wedding day she would stand without them to support her friend.

'Anna insisted on a "proper" bridesmaid's dress,' Sandra said laughingly, 'even though I've tried to explain what a quiet wedding means. Fortunately Leo had no desire whatever to be a page boy.'

Principally because it was to be a quiet affair, but also

because she had been married before, Sandra had decided on a simple outfit, a fitted dress and coat in a creamy self-patterned material. The small matching hat did not obscure her radiant face and for a bouquet she carried a small spray of sweet-scented freesias.

'You look beautiful,' Sandra's father told her proudly as they waited in the vicarage parlour. 'Almost,' with a twinkle at his wife who was making last-minute adjustments to the tilt of Sandra's hat, 'almost but not quite as beautiful as your mother.'

Sandra hugged his arm.

'And if Griff is only nine-tenths the husband and father you've been I shall be the luckiest woman alive,' she returned the compliment.

Having finally succeeded in hustling his wife on her way to the church, Andrew Lessing led his daughter from the front door of the vicarage and along the road to the lychgate. They could have used the private entrance between house and church, but the whole village had turned out to see the wedding and Sandra didn't want to deprive them of their moment of enjoyment.

In the porch Anna and Amber awaited them, Amber in her wheelchair which was pushed up the aisle behind the bride until the little party reached the altar, when Amber stood to receive Sandra's bouquet.

A beaming Bert Bradshaw had been pressed into service as best man while the rest of the staff from the Manor occupied the family pew, and Sandra knew a moment of sadness that Molly Faversham wasn't there to share in the general happiness. Griff must feel it too, she thought, as she looked up at him, tall and unfamiliar-looking in his best suit.

Then she met his eyes, saw the light shining in them, and knew that at this moment his thoughts were concentrated upon her and their love for each other. In

Less than an hour this man would be her husband, with all that implied, and before this day was out they would at last be truly one. From that moment the solemn words of the marriage service, their responses to each other and to the clergyman seemed to take place in a golden haze that was not altogether imaginary. For the sun had chosen that moment to glance in through a Gothic-arched stained-glass window above the altar and a medley of rainbow colours enclosed bride and groom in their warm aura.

St Thomas's possessed no organ of its own, but somehow the ancient harmonium from the vicarage parlour had been manhandled across to the church and a beaming Nonie rendered the Wedding March as bride and groom came down the aisle.

Griff had insisted that there must be proper photographs.

'Not that I'll need them to remember our wedding day,' he had told Sandra with tender earnestness, 'but it will be something to show our children—our other children!' he added unnecessarily, making her blush.

Amber and Nonie, in a new accord that was good to see, had insisted on supplying the wedding breakfast, and after bride and groom had run the gamut of good wishes and confetti showered upon them by guests and onlookers alike, the small party gathered at the vicarage.

'I suppose it's no good asking where you're going to spend your honeymoon?' Amber teased when it was almost time for the newly-weds to leave.

'No use whatever,' Griff confirmed.

The twins had been more than a little dismayed to find that they were not to accompany their mother and their adored Uncle Griff on this 'special holiday', and Leo at least looked a little tearful. But as the twins were to spend the next fortnight with their grandparents, Sandra had no worries about them. Leo had been a changed child since the night he confided his terrors to Griff, and if it were possible to love her husband more than she already did, it must have been because of his understanding and tactful handling of her children.

'What is it they say on occasions like this?' Griff joked as he ushered her into his car which someone had found time to adorn with slogans and rattling tin cans. 'Alone at last! It's a pity,' he said throatily, 'that we've got a couple of hours' drive ahead of us, before we . . .'

'I could almost wish we were staying here,' Sandra said as they came in sight of the Manor House. They had returned to collect an item of Griff's luggage that had inadvertently been left out of the boot of his car. 'Not that I'm not looking forward to Cornwall,' she added hastily—she had insisted on not going abroad. 'But . . .'

'But?' he asked her as they went upstairs to his room.

Sandra blushed and shook her head, letting her hair fall forward in a familiar gesture to hid her rosy cheeks.

'No. You'll think me silly and . . . and forward.'

'Forward!' Griff said incredulously. 'That'll be the day! How long did it take me to get you even to admit that you loved me? I insist on hearing your "but".'

Her face still hidden from him, she said the words so softly that even with his head inclined he could not hear them and had to insist that she repeated them.

'I said,' her voice was husky, tremulous, 'I would have liked the first time you made love to me to be here, in our own house, in . . . in our own room. I've imagined it so often.'

She waited for him to dismiss the idea or, even worse to laugh at her. So she was totally unprepared for his tenderness when he took her in his arms. A fierce flame burned in his eyes as he said, 'Whatever you ask of me, my darling Sandra, it shall be yours. If that's what you want then it's what I want too. Hell, who am I kidding?' he demanded throatily. 'I've been wondering how I was going to wait until we got to Cornwall. Now I find you feel the same way.' His arms tightened. 'We *will* make love, here, now.' He released her briefly, long enough to close the bedroom door and turn the key in the lock.'

'Are you sure?' A delicious shiver tremored through her. 'But what about . . .?'

'And if you're worried about the servants, don't be,' he said as he moved towards her. 'I told them to stay on at the vicarage until the end of the party, which won't be yet, I fancy. So, Mrs Faversham, how about it? Or are you having second thoughts?' The words were humorous but his voice was huskily intense.

'No second thoughts,' she assured him. She stood on tiptoe reached up and pulled his head down to hers, then kissed him, opening the soft warmth of her mouth to him, arching towards him in simple unmistakable offering. He pulled her to him, his hard body pressed against her, making her aware of his throbbing desire. The tip of his tongue eased her lips apart. She clung to him, her fervour equal to his, her arms straining tightly about his neck.

'God, I needed that!' As his lips freed hers his breathing was ragged. 'Sometimes in the last month I've thought today would never come, wished we hadn't promised each other we'd wait.'

'It was worth it. And now the waiting's over,' she told him, as she began to slip the jacket of his suit from his shoulders. Her fingers trembled as she unbuttoned his shirt so that she could run her fingers over his taut, warm skin, the sensation exciting her as much as it did him.

'I love you, Griff,' she whispered feverishly against his neck.

'Sandra.' His voice was a strangled sound. 'I seem to have been waiting a lifetime to hear you say that. God knows how much I love you, how much I want you, now and always. I don't think I'll ever be able to have enough of you.'

She slid her fingers over the firm contours of his shoulders and down over his muscular back, slowly exploring the delineation of his spine until she reached its base. She felt the swift inhalation of his breath.

'I was afraid at first to let myself fall in love with you,' she told him. 'But I do. I *love* you, Griff,' she repeated wonderingly, happiness flooding through her anew, 'so much that I can't believe this is really happening. I want you, too.' She had never wanted anything so much in all her life. No courage was needed now. With confidence she continued to caress him, eased her fingers beneath the waistband of his trousers.

She felt the zip of her dress give way to his importunate fingers. It slid to the floor, followed by the simple slip she wore. She heard him give a shuddering gasp as he discovered she wore no bra; her firm contours needed no support. He bent his head so that his mouth could capture the swelling peaks of her breasts. First his lips and then his teeth made a gentle erotic exploration, a sensation almost intolerably exquisite.

'Griff!' she implored, felt the negatory movement of his head.

'Not yet. I've waited a long time for this,' he murmured. 'But I'm not going to rush it, or you.' But he held her close against him as though he would never let her go. Feeling his urgency, she could only marvel at his control that now seemed to exceed her own as he caressed her, touching and arousing until she thought she must die of the need he was awaking within her, yet still refused to satisfy.

Deftly he discarded his own clothes then removed the flimsy scrap of lace that was all that remained of her underwear. They stood naked in each other's arms. The masculine strength, the nearness of him were an aching torture and her body burned to know his.

At last when she thought she could stand no more, he lifted her on to the bed and came down beside her. With a sigh of blissful contentment she melded herself to him, revelling in the knowledge of her effect upon him as he shuddered against her. He was breathing hard as though he had been running. Yet still he was in control, considerate of her.

'Sandra?' he questioned gently.

'Yes, Griff, oh yes, please, love me. I want you so badly.'

His mouth claimed hers again in a kiss of intense need, leaving her pliant and trembling. As he curved his hands about her hips, raising her, she slid her arms round his neck, plunging her hands into the virile growth of his hair to bring his head down to hers once more. There was a pulsating ache in the lower half of her body, an ache for which there was only one satisfactory cure.

With one supple move, he positioned himself over her and at last, with a wondering sigh, she knew the feel of him inside her. His movements were slow at first, but as she urged against him, crying out his name, her love for him, the momentum increased, heightening the pleasurable torment. Then deep, deep inside her there came an explosive, pleasurable release, a release he shared, deep, tender, sublimely passionate, as their bodies, minds and spirits met in total sympathy.

Coming Next Month

2977 RANSOMED HEART Ann Charlton

Hal Stevens, hired by her wealthy father to protect Stacey, wastes no time in letting her know he considers her a spoiled brat and her life-style useless. But Stacey learns that even heiresses can't have everything they want....

2978 SONG OF LOVE Rachel Elliott

Claire Silver hadn't known Roddy Mackenzie very long—yet staying in his Scottish castle was just long enough to fall in love with him. Then suddenly Roddy is treating her as if he thinks she's using him. Has he had a change of heart?

2979 THE WILD SIDE Diana Hamilton

Hannah should have been on holiday in Morocco. Instead, she finds herself kidnapped to a snowbound cottage in Norfolk by a total stranger. And yet Waldo Ross seems to know all about Hannah.

2980 WITHOUT RAINBOWS Virginia Hart

Penny intends to persuade her father, Lon, to give up his dangerous obsession with treasure hunting. She *doesn't* intend to fall in love with Steffan Korda again—especially since he's financing Lon's next expedition in the Greek islands.

2981 ALIEN MOONLIGHT Kate Kingston

Petra welcomes the temporary job as nanny to three children in France as an escape from her ex-fiancé's attentions. She hasn't counted on Adam Herrald, the children's uncle. Sparks fly whenever they meet. But why does he dislike her?

2982 WHEN THE LOVING STOPPED Jessica Steele

It is entirely Whitney's fault that businessman Sloan Illingworth's engagement has ended disastrously. It seems only fair that she should make amends. Expecting her to take his fiancée's place in his life, however, seems going a bit too far!

Available in May wherever paperback books are sold, or through Harlequin Reader Service:

In the U.S.	In Canada
901 Fuhrmann Blvd.	P.O. Box 603
P.O. Box 1397	Fort Erie, Ontario
Buffalo, N.Y. 14240-1397	L2A 5X3

"GIVE YOUR HEART TO HARLEQUIN" SWEEPSTAKES

OFFICIAL RULES

NO PURCHASE NECESSARY TO ENTER OR RECEIVE A PRIZE

1. To enter and join the Harlequin Reader Service, rub off the concealment device on all game tickets. This will reveal the values for each Sweepstakes entry number and the number of free books you will receive. Accepting the free books will automatically entitle you to also receive a free bonus gift. If you do not wish to take advantage of our introduction to the Harlequin Reader Service but wish to enter the Sweepstakes only, rub off the concealment device on tickets #1-3 only. To enter, return your entire sheet of tickets. Incomplete and/or inaccurate entries are not eligible for that section or sections of prizes. Not responsible for mutilated or unreadable entries or inadvertent printing errors. Mechanically reproduced entries are null and void.

2. Either way, your Sweepstakes numbers will be compared against the list of winning numbers generated at random by computer. In the event that all prizes are not claimed, random drawings will be held from all entries received from all presentations to award all unclaimed prizes. All cash prizes are payable in U.S. funds. This is in addition to any free, surprise or mystery gifts that might be offered. The following prizes are awarded in this sweepstakes:

(1)	*Grand Prize	$1,000,000	Annuity
(1)	First Prize	$35,000	
(1)	Second Prize	$10,000	
(3)	Third Prize	$5,000	
(10)	Fourth Prize	$1,000	
(25)	Fifth Prize	$500	
(5000)	Sixth Prize	$5	

*The Grand Prize is payable through a $1,000,000 annuity. Winner may elect to receive $25,000 a year for 40 years, totaling up to $1,000,000 without interest, or $350,000 in one cash payment. Winners selected will receive the prizes offered in the Sweepstakes promotion they receive.
Entrants may cancel the Reader Service at any time without cost or obligation to buy (see details in center insert card).

3. Versions of this Sweepstakes with different graphics may appear in other mailings or at retail outlets by Torstar Corp. and its affiliates. This promotion is being conducted under the supervision of Marden-Kane, Inc., an independent judging organization. By entering the Sweepstakes, each entrant accepts and agrees to be bound by these rules and the decisions of the judges, which shall be final and binding. Odds of winning are dependent upon the total number of entries received. Taxes, if any, are the sole responsibility of the winners. Prizes are nontransferable. All entries must be received by March 31, 1990. The drawing will take place on April 30, 1990, at the offices of Marden-Kane, Inc., Lake Success, N.Y.

4. This offer is open to residents of the U.S., Great Britain and Canada, 18 years or older, except employees of Torstar Corp., its affiliates, and subsidiaries, Marden-Kane, Inc. and all other agencies and persons connected with conducting this Sweepstakes. All federal, state and local laws apply. Void wherever prohibited or restricted by law.

5. Winners will be notified by mail and may be required to execute an affidavit of eligibility and release that must be returned within 14 days after notification. Canadian winners will be required to answer a skill-testing question. Winners consent to the use of their name, photograph and/or likeness for advertising and publicity in conjunction with this and similar promotions without additional compensation. One prize per family or household.

6. For a list of our most current major prizewinners, send a stamped, self-addressed envelope to: WINNERS LIST, c/o MARDEN-KANE, INC., P.O. BOX 701, SAYREVILLE, N.J. 08872

LTY-H49